OUT OF THE NIGHT

THE EPIC STORY OF RJ AND YORK
BOOK ONE

SUSAN MAY WARREN

Soli Deo Gloria

For the fans of the Montana Marshalls.
You make storytelling fun.

OUT OF THE NIGHT

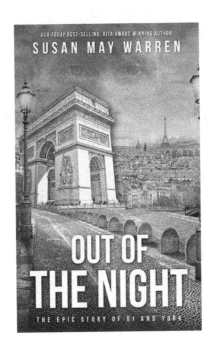

All former spy and current national security agent York Newgate wants is to propose to the woman he loves, RJ

Marshall. Then they can move to Shelly, Washington, and start the calm, safe life he's been dreaming of for over a year.

Too bad trouble doesn't agree.

Or maybe RJ simply attracts trouble because she's just going out for coffee when she spots a wanted, known terrorist standing in the middle of a street in Paris. At least she *thinks* it's international criminal Alan Martin, the mastermind behind a plot to kill the president.

But he's in jail, right?

Wrong. Martin has escaped, and it's up to RJ—and York—to keep him in their sights until he can be apprehended. But chasing down Martin means following him into the darkness of whatever plot he's cooked up now.

So much for York's epic proposal. Now, he just wants to escape Europe with their lives.

The epic romantic trilogy ignites!

CHAPTER
ONE

York wasn't a coward. Not even a little. Besides, RJ was going to say yes.

It was just that he wanted it to be perfect. In every way—from the ambiance, to the food, the stroll along the Seine under a twinkle-light sky, even down to the buskers singing romantic French songs.

Everything had been meticulously planned and was now aligned for the moment he got down on one knee and asked Ruby Jane Marshall to marry him. Finally.

And really, that was the only reason it had taken him so very long—painfully, ridiculously, stupidly long for him to propose. Because after a year and a half of chasing down bad guys—namely, a plot to kill the president by one former vice-president, which included checking and rechecking their evidence for the federal prosecutor—he was so very ready to make good on his promise to return to small town Shelly, Montana, and build a life together.

One that included a front porch view of Lake Shelly, via the gorgeous timber-framed house he'd put an offer on—a surprise wedding gift for RJ.

Yes, York had it all figured out. Once they'd gotten clear of the trial, he'd booked this trip to Paris, purchased a beautiful vintage two carat diamond ring, made dinner reservations at the famed Le Jules Verne restaurant at the Eiffel Tower, with the glittering lights of Paris sprayed at their footsteps. And tonight, during their romantic after dinner walk, he'd tell her how she'd changed his life.

How, somehow, despite his losses, the wounds, she'd healed him.

Most of all, that he couldn't wait one more minute to marry her, if she'd have him. In his mind's eye, she said yes, of course, and leaped into his arms, and—

It would all end happily, he knew it in his heart.

He just had to get to the restaurant in time. Which meant getting through the massive crowd that thronged the entrance to grand, historic Hôtel Le Bristol.

"Are you kidding me?" RJ said next to him, her hand in his. Oh, she looked devastatingly beautiful tonight, her dark hair back in a smooth, elegant roll, wearing a black dress, low heels, a pair of diamond earrings he'd given her for Christmas. She smelled amazing—a floral scent that lingered throughout their two-bedroom suite.

He was going to behave himself tonight. Absolutely.

But he was growing tired of the longing to have her in his bed, waking up to her every morning. The longing to make permanent what he felt in his heart.

He wanted RJ as his wife.

"I know, it's amazing, isn't it?" he said as they walked through the lobby. The checkered black and white travertine floors, the orange trees in planters that lined the room, the French revival style furniture, the three-Michelin star restaurant, and especially the courtyard garden. He'd been here once, long ago, with the daughter of the US Ambassador to Russia, and despite how that turned out, the place held romance in the air.

"It is—how did you know that Winchester Marshall would be here?" Ruby Jane tugged on his hand as they headed toward the crowd, pushing against a roped off red carpet that trekked from a hotel ballroom out to the street.

"Who?"

But one look at the massive movie poster that dangled over the beautiful century old doors, he could guess.

Winchester Marshall, actor, in his newest American spy flick. He played Jack Powers, a slick ex-CIA agent. York could admit, up on the wall like that, the guy looked impressive—dark hair, blue eyes, built. But probably that was all photo shopped and besides, the guy didn't have the first clue what it took to really get into the spy game.

You didn't end up with a pretty face, and an unadulterated smile. For a second, he was keenly aware of the scar that ran from his ear to his jaw.

And then, he shrugged it away. He wasn't competing with this joker—

"Let's see if we can see him."

He looked at her. "RJ—"

She turned back. Cocked her head. "Yeah, you're right. I'm being silly. It's just that there's lore in the family that he's a distant cousin, so..." She lifted a shoulder.

"If you want to stay..."

"No. I want to go. I'm starved."

He wrapped an arm around her neck and kissed her temple. "I have an amazing dinner planned."

He'd ordered a car, but it took an extra tip to the doorman to get the car close enough—Marshall's crowd clogged the street in front of the entrance, and in the end, they had to wait until the actor emerged—to a ridiculous amount of wild fanfare—and got in his limo before their Uber could pull up.

As it were, he and RJ got a glimpse of the man as he waved to the crowd. He looked every inch the man on his stupid poster, dark hair perfectly in place, a chiseled jaw, flashing blue eyes, and under that black tuxedo, a physique he'd earned in a gym.

Instead of the steely world of actual hard work.

"I'll bet he's on the way to his premiere," RJ said. "I heard it's an international tour. I can't wait to see the movie. Brr. I'm cold. Are you cold?"

Actually, he'd broken a sweat, his other hand in his pocket, wrapped around the tiny velveteen box. The last thing he needed was a pickpocket.

They got into their Uber, he confirmed the address and then he sat back, his arm around RJ.

She fit perfectly against him.

He almost asked her right then, with the lights of Paris in her eyes. As they drove past the Champs-Elysees, then the Flame of Liberty Memorial—the statue that duplicated their own statue of liberty—and then across the river and toward the Eiffel Tower.

Lights glittered from the Eiffel Tower as twilight fell over the city. Romance, hope, their future seasoned in the summer air.

He didn't deserve the second chance, but he wasn't going to waste it.

"It's gorgeous," RJ said.

"Mmmhmm."

They got out at the park, and he took her hand, so as not to lose her in the maddening crowd that jammed the base of the tower. Apparently, dinner hour was the high time to visit the tower.

They headed to the south pillar entrance, to the private elevator there. Even here, a crowd pushed around the entrance. Cameras flashed.

He wove his way to the front, where a bouncer blocked the door.

"Hello," York said, and the man frowned, so he switched to French. "I have dinner reservations."

"Are you with Premier Events?"

Now York raised an eyebrow. "No. But I have a confirmation number." He reached for his phone to pull it up.

"Not tonight you don't," the man said. Not a big man, but he wore an air about him that suggested he didn't take much in the way of argument.

"Yes, tonight I do," York said and let go of RJ's hand to scroll through the phone.

Behind him, screams and cheers lifted off the crowd.

"He's here," RJ said, and York looked up from his scrolling through his emails to see, oh perfect, Winchester Marshall in the flesh parting the crowd, working his way to the door, waving, smiling, flanked by a couple security people and a few others in his entourage.

They reached the door, and the bouncer stepped in front of York to push him back as Marshall stood at the entrance, waved again, smiling that thousand-watt smile, and headed inside.

The door closed.

Oh.

What?

He turned back to his phone, did a quick search, and landed on an unopened email.

Dated two weeks ago.

He opened it, and his gut clenched.

"Did you find your reservation?" the bouncer asked.

York nodded, his jaw tight. "It's been canceled."

The man shrugged. "Tomorrow night, perhaps?"

Probably not. In the email it gave him an option to reschedule. Which he hadn't, of course.

He blew out a breath and another actor showed up and the crowd again erupted.

"That's Lincoln Cash," RJ said, even as she grabbed his arm and pulled him away from the entrance.

"Who?"

The man was tall—maybe 6'4", with blond hair, lines around his blue eyes, but still someone who looked like they should be on some Hollywood A-list.

"He was an actor, but quit and started directing. He's done all the Jack Powers movies, and turned the franchise into more than just a spy movie, but really deepened the character, given him a story."

Cheers as the man turned and waved to the crowd, like he might be a superhero.

"Let's get out of here," he said. "We need to find a place to eat."

She looked over at him. "I'm sorry about the reservations."

He lifted a shoulder. But this was their life, it seemed—too busy to catch up to their dreams, to grab a hold.

"I should have seen the email," he said as they worked their way back to the street.

"We can find somewhere else." She wove her fingers through his. "I thought I saw a French pizza place on our drive over."

Perfect. Yes, that's what he wanted—to propose over a pepperoni and mushroom pizza.

He sighed.

"Are you okay?"

Overhead, stars spilled out across the velvet sky, and fell upon the river, which lapped against the walkway. Lamps on the bridge had flickered on.

They passed other couples out for a stroll, families, a few people wandering alone, some focused on their phones.

In the distance, the city started to glow against the pane of night.

Maybe he should just take a breath. So the night hadn't gone as he'd wanted. It could still be perfect, here, on the bridge, with the city of romance as a backdrop.

He turned to her.

The wind off the Seine had caught her hair, and a strand twined around her face. He caught it and tucked it behind her ear, let his fingers rest on her cheek. "You take my breath away."

She blinked at him, smiled, her blue eyes deepening. "York. You're such a romantic."

He didn't feel romantic. Most of the time his brain buzzed with what-ifs, his body strung with a sort of tension that he hadn't been able to shake since marine boot-camp. The only time he remembered slowing down enough to breathe, to blink and sink into life had been when his memory went on hiatus for a month and he'd become Mack Jones, small town cook and bartender.

But even then, he'd gotten into a couple scuffles, and had saved his boss's life by diving into a burning building, so he couldn't really count that as, you know, slowing down.

Still, here, tonight, with just their future ahead of them, yes, he could let himself listen to his heart. Taste his dreams.

Grab the happy ending he'd been working for.

"You make it easy," he said, leaning in and kissing her. She tasted of wholeness, of belonging, a familiarity and yet a passion in her touch that sparked desire deep in his core.

A hand on his chest made him pull away. Probably a good thing because his heart was hammering. She smiled up at him. "Again, I ask, are you okay?"

"Finally," he said, and she frowned.

"It's just been such a long...year. With the Jackson conspiracy and trial and...well, I finally get you to myself."

"So that's what this trip is about." She pulled out her phone, and stepped up to him, turned her back to him. "Selfie in Paris."

He smiled, something half-hearted, even as she grinned. She snapped the shot and then sent it somewhere. Maybe Facebook.

Then, she pocketed the phone, took a step close and slid her arms into his jacket, around him. "Here I am, all yours."

All yours. Yes. He took a breath, stepped away and took her hands.

Now.

Yes. Under a perfect Paris night sky, with the wind stirring up the scent of summer flowers and that look in her eyes.

He started to kneel—

A scream ripped through the night.

RJ jerked away from him, turning, probably reflex.

He too stood up.

Another scream. It came from below the bridge, along the river walk and they pressed against the cement railing.

A woman and man had scooted down the bank and were reaching into the water toward—

"Is that a body?" RJ said.

York gave a grim nod.

"We should help." And of course, she took off down the bridge.

Perfect.

He followed her down to the edge of the river where, by the time he arrived, a small crowd had gathered. Someone had dragged the body—a woman—to shore, turned her over and a man had started CPR.

There wasn't a chance. She was already gray, and in a moment when the body refused to respond, he stopped.

Behind them, a siren whined, cutting through the night.

"How terrible," RJ said, even as she vied for a better look. "I wonder if she jumped."

Then, to his horror, she took out her phone and took a shot of the body.

"What. Are you. *Doing*?" He grabbed her back, even as the police agents came down the embankment.

"I..." She looked at him. "I don't know. Habit?"

He sighed. As a former CIA analyst, those instincts were probably embedded in her.

Except, he wasn't exactly muting the what-ifs that suddenly stirred in his brain. What if she jumped? What if she was pushed? Accident, suicide or...murder?

So maybe they both had a hard time shutting down their brains.

RJ wrinkled her nose at him. "Sorry." She turned back to the scene, even as the agents pulled her further onto shore, told people to get back.

He glanced at the woman. Hard to tell her age, but maybe early forties, dark hair, and she wore dress pants and a blouse, as if she'd come from work. No shoes, but her feet were bare, so maybe she'd had on heels.

No visible marks, but that didn't mean anything, really.

Stop.

The smell of the body rose and he grabbed RJ and pulled

her away. Now his stomach soured, and so much for the romantic night.

"Pizza?" He helped her up the embankment.

"Sounds perfect." She slipped her hand into his.

Not yet. But sometime in the next five days, it would be.

It would help if her brain didn't latch onto every scenario and spin it out of control. Or if the lights of Paris nightlife didn't spray into her room like neon. And of course, there was the memory of York, weirdly pensive and quiet as they'd eaten pizza at a quaint, delightful street cafe late in the night. The city buzzed around them, even at the late hour and with it her entire body.

RJ loved this life. Loved the fact that York had booked them this trip to Paris, and sure, he was right—they needed some breathing space after the last year investigating and shutting the case on former VP-elect Reba Jackson and her assassination plot against current President Isaac White.

But how did he expect her to simply...relax? They were in *La Ville Lumière* —the city of lights, of love, of spy novels and revolutionaries and history and...

Mystery.

No, sleep was for the dead. Or maybe a beach somewhere, but she wasn't going to miss one second of adventure in the exotic city of Paris. RJ got up and threw back the rose tapestry drapes. The view opened to a balcony that overlooked the cityscape.

The room was huge—a king size bed, a writing desk, a dresser, a spray of fresh red roses on the bureau. And dripping down from the ceiling, in the middle of an ornate medallion, the most gorgeous gold and crystal glass chandelier she'd ever seen. What York spent on their two-bedroom guest suite she didn't want to guess.

But she felt like Marie Antoinette, a little pampered by all this elegance.

In fact, deep in her heart, she hoped that York might be proposing. Of course, they'd talked about marriage—often, really. At least in the beginning, when they'd first moved to Shelly, Washington, where he'd lived as a man named Mack Jones.

She lived in a cute Victorian—he'd taken a flat over a bar and grill where he sometimes worked. Part of his small-town alias.

All the while, they sleuthed out the truth about Jackson, connecting her not only to a string of murders, but a dating service app that turned out to be a connection for hired assassins. And then, of course, she'd tried to bomb one of White's Inaugural Day parties.

They'd traced her dealings all the way back to a Russian connection with one Arkady Petrov, a hard-liner General who ran a branch of the Bratva, a man who wanted to reignite a cold war.

A cold war meant weapons, which meant money, and as a stockholder, Jackson was poised to make billions, even as she helmed the country as the first female president. And it had all been orchestrated by a man named Alan Martin, the same man who'd tried to kill York and left him for dead.

A man securely behind federal bars in Washington D.C.

So that had consumed most of their time and energy and after a few months, York had stopped talking about marriage.

Or maybe...

She drew in a breath, the air smelling of the city, a mix of bakery and cobblestone, the noise of the morning traffic stirring off the nearby street, even seven stories up.

What if he didn't want to get married anymore? What if he was happy with their, um, relationship?

What if he just wanted a partner, as in the work version? Despite the kiss he'd given her on the bridge—a kiss so thorough, so focused, maybe even vulnerable, that she thought, crazily, that he might be about to propose.

But then came the body, the pizza, a quiet walk home and he hadn't exactly made any extra moves last night when he bid her goodnight at her door.

Not that he would. Sure, he'd practically kidnapped her the first time he'd met her, but that had been to save her life. The man had always been nothing but...well, a gentleman.

Okay, sometimes he broke through that suave 007 veneer, but most of the time she felt his carefully banked passion.

But what if...what if that's all he wanted to give?

She closed her bathroom door and turned on the shower. He'd already lost a wife and a child. And his last girlfriend had been murdered—either by an assassin, or by a former CIA operative, a double agent co-worker.

She got in the shower.

So, yes, she got it—why he might be hesitant to step into something permanent, something that could eviscerate him if their work followed them home.

Ah, see, there went her imagination, working overtime. She was just seeing his face as he stared at that dead woman last night.

White. A little horror, and she'd instantly regretted following her curiosity down to the riverbank. No need to dig up reminders of the past.

No, she didn't want to ask for more if he wasn't ready to go there. She loved him enough to wait. And, in the meantime, to chase down adventure in Paris, or wherever it brought them.

She got out of the shower, toweled off and headed back out to the bedroom. Pulling on a sundress, she slipped into flats and simply tied up her damp hair. The hotel offered a wide array of tea, but despite York's palate she couldn't abide the stuff.

A quick scoot to the coffee shop down the street and she'd be right back.

She stepped out into the living area and cast a look over to York's closed door. Considered knocking. But maybe the guy needed his sleep. Maybe she'd score some croissants for breakfast while she was out and they could eat them on the balcony, at the cute bistro table.

She was in the lobby before she thought of her phone, still charging on the desk in her room. Oops.

The lobby was quiet at this early hour, the throngs from last night gone, just a few businessmen with roller bags or seated on the sofas with morning brews, reading their phones. A line extended from the hotel coffee shop.

She slipped outside, smiled at the doorman and headed down the street. A flock of pigeons scattered off the sidewalk, and a few scooters motored by. She'd spotted a bistro with a coffee cup etched on the window when they'd arrived yesterday, and now found the place half-full of morning customers, the seats outside occupied by people drinking their coffee. Most of them were glued to their phones, so she queued up behind a petite girl who had 'French' written all over her in her *haute couture* sun dress and heels. RJ felt like a hillbilly next to her.

Especially when a handsome man, dark hair, wearing a baseball cap and dark glasses queued up behind her. He didn't even look at her as she smiled at him, his attention on his phone.

American.

Another man—definitely American, by the look of his jeans, boots, aviator glasses and short clipped brown hair, slipped into the shop and got in line. He lifted his chin, nodding at her in acknowledgment before she turned back around.

Yikes. Apparently, she stood out.

The place smelled deliciously of dark roast coffee, and the floor squeaked appropriately as they moved forward. A few patrons sat in the leather chairs inside, but most took their brew outside in fat wide cups, some holding treats from the glass case.

She was eying a rather large chocolate croissant with her name on it when—bam! The man behind her smacked into her. Flying forward, she slammed into the French girl, who then bumped the man in front of her, just retrieving his coffee.

The entire domino effect sent the coffee flying into the wait staff and across the counter.

Whoops.

Angry Parisian man rounded on fashionable Parisian girl who looked at RJ and rattled off something in furious French, and RJ could do nothing but to turn to the jerk behind her who—

Wait.

Winchester Marshall?

She froze, even as he made a face at her.

"Sorry. I thought you moved forward."

She gestured to the angry French people behind her, and he raised his hand. "Again, sorry."

The barrage of French continued and in a terrible second, a wait person rounded the end of the counter and suddenly, she found herself ousted from the café, tumbling out with the A-list actor on her heels.

"Huh." He stood there, surrounded by the clutter of patrons, who barely looked at him. "I didn't expect that."

"I'll bet not." She turned away from the café. "Now where am I going to get coffee?"

"There's another little shop down the street," he said. "I found it yesterday when this line was too long."

She looked at him. "I certainly hope you're buying, Bigfoot."

He stared at her. And then, a slow smile slipped up his face. He brought his glasses down. A beat passed between them.

"I guess I am." He put the glasses back on. "I'm—"

"I know who you are. But you probably don't know me. I'm Ruby Jane Marshall." She held out her hand.

He took it. "Marshall?"

"I think we're, um…okay, I know you probably get this a lot, but really, it's the truth—we're related. My father was Orrin Marshall."

He held her hand, nodding. "Wait—as in John and Orrin Marshall?"

"John was my father's brother, but yes…"

"My father, Patrick, is their cousin."

"Mmmhmm."

"So that makes us, what—?"

"Second cousins?" she said. They started walking down the street.

"Isn't that called kissing cousins?" He had a thousand-watt smile, and despite their family connection, he was utterly charming.

"Don't get any bright ideas there, superstar. I'm taken."

"Figures." But he laughed, and she did too.

They'd walked about a half block when in a passing

window she spotted the man she'd seen in the coffee shop following them.

"You have a stalker," she said quietly.

He glanced over his shoulder, then laughed. "That's Lake. Personal security. My publicist insisted."

Personal security. Huh.

Here she was, with Winchester Marshall. Walking down the street with Winchester Marshall, second cousin, movie star—no, walking down a *Paris* street with Winchester Marshall, second cousin, movie star, with *personal security*.

Yep, this was her life.

They passed planters overflowing with all color of pansies, historic buildings with dark mansard roofs that had probably housed some famous sculptor or painter. Past cafés with Parisians drinking coffee, eating croissants.

"So, you visiting, or—"

"Visiting. With my boyfriend. I'm from Montana, although, I currently live in Washington state."

"Huh. Me too. I have a ranch near Bozeman."

"Really? We live near Geraldine."

He glanced at her. "Really." They'd reached the café, and he held the door open for her.

This place had a different vibe, very trendy with the sounds of espresso shots being pulled pinging off the tile floor. Tall stainless-steel roasters in the back were cordoned off by glass. They parked themselves in the long line. "Maybe I should visit."

"Oh, you definitely should visit," she said.

"I grew up in Florida. We visited cousins in Minnesota once."

"Uncle John's kids. They're great."

He nodded. "Actually, their oldest, Fraser, and I kept in touch. Great guy. A SEAL."

"Former SEAL. But yeah."

"So, what do you do?" They had moved up in the line.

"I...um...I'm an analyst. I sleuth out possible threats for a private group." Really, she'd never quite figured out how to unpack what she did for the Caleb Group, a security task force formed by President Isaac White.

What she really wanted to do, however, was, well, this. Travel the world, track down evil and stop it.

"A 'three-letter' group?" He finger quoted the words.

"If you mean the CIA, then no." Or, at least not anymore.

He laughed. "Yeah. Even if you did, you couldn't tell me, right?"

She shook her head. "It's not exciting. I study reports and then write reports."

"Ah, the stock market. You're one of the smart ones."

Her face heated, but she nodded. Leave it at that, maybe.

"So, why did your boyfriend bring you to the city of loooove?" He raised an eyebrow.

Oh. They stepped up to the counter. "I'll have an Americano, and..." He looked at her, and now took down his glasses, and raised a handsome eyebrow.

"A latte."

"A latte." He peeled off the appropriate number of euros and they moved to the counter to wait.

"We just finished a big project and I think he wanted to celebrate. Actually, my, um, boyfriend had reservations at the Le Jules Verne last night. They got bumped for your private party."

He made a face. "Sorry."

"We ended up at this cute pizza place. It was fine."

"Still. The Jules Verne has a great view of the city. Tell him I'm sorry—and if there's anything I can do to make it up to him..."

The barista called their order and set their cups on the shelf.

Oops. Cute white ceramic *not* to-go cups. And next to the cups, a couple chocolate croissants.

"Uh...oh..."

"I saw you eying them." He had tucked his glasses away and now gave her a wink.

Oh, he was a charmer.

"Mind if we eat outside?" He took the tray and carried it out to the street where he found a free table away from traffic and under an umbrella. He somehow squeezed that body into a chair, and she felt like paparazzi should show up, their lights flashing.

What. Ever.

"So, what's on your sight-seeing list?" He took his coffee and balanced it in his very big, capable, elegant hands.

"Um. I don't know. Versailles, I guess? And maybe the Louvre?"

"Only if you like thousands of sculptures of naked people." She had picked up her cup, and now raised an eyebrow.

"The Louv-R is not G-rated." He said it with a pronounced R on the end.

Um.

"The first time I went, there was a crowd so thick around the Mona Lisa—which, by the way is about as big as an 8 x 10 picture—that I had to use binoculars to see it. Mind you, I was fifteen, but still. My mom just had to take us there. My dad called it the Louv-R, so it sorta stuck." He gave a shudder. "Talk about being deeply scarred. Not all those naked women should have their clothing off, if you know what I mean."

"There were different standards of beauty through the ages."

He put his cup down. "Couz, there's only one standard of beauty. And that's in the eyes of the beholder, right?"

She liked him. She'd seen a few interviews on television, and he'd always seemed funny. Sweet. But in the flesh, he was just a nice guy.

Who looked like the super spy he played in the movies.

She suppressed a chuckle, thinking about York and his opinion of the Jack Powers movies.

"What?" Winchester Marshall, The Beautiful said.

She made to open her mouth, closed it. Then, "Nothing."

"You were far away, thinking of something. What was it?"

She lifted a shoulder. "Just...I...let's just say that I know a guy who actually does...what Jack Powers does. And I wonder what he'd think about me sitting here with you."

"I hope that guy you know would think, hey, it's a family reunion. Nothing to see here."

She nodded. "Yep. Probably." Not even a little.

"So, your boyfriend is a spy, huh?"

She looked at him. "I didn't say that—"

"And you're here for some clandestine mission." He leaned forward, lowered his voice. "So, who are we staking out?"

"We're not—"

"How about that couple over there?" He nodded with his chin to a woman in heels, wearing a floral dress, and her counterpart, a man in skinny jeans and a button-down shirt. They wore sunglasses and drank their coffee in silence.

"Naw. They're just a couple trying to figure out how to ask for a divorce."

"Oh, maudlin, are we?"

She lifted a shoulder.

"Okay, maybe that's our target?" He pointed to a woman securing her bike to a post. She wore skinny jeans, sandals, a backpack over her floral blouse.

"Courier. Not the package."

He made a face, lips drawn down. "Now we're getting somewhere." He turned to look at the crowd, then pointed to a man across the street. "What about him?"

He stood staring at the café, his dark glasses not betraying exactly at whom, but the moment RJ looked at him, a chill skittered through her. Sure, he was across traffic, but his build, that short dark hair, the way he just stood, staring at...wait, her?...

Alan Martin.

No. It couldn't be.

But he had the build, the short dark hair...the scar that traced his forehead.

Her breath caught.

"Are you okay?"

She looked down and found that she'd spilled coffee on her shirt. Now she set the cup on the table, her hands trembling.

Picked up a napkin and glanced back at the man.

Gone.

"You look like you saw, I dunno, an ex, walking with your best friend."

She looked at him. "I don't have exes."

"Lucky." But still he frowned. "And you're a little pale."

"I...It's been super great to meet you, Winchester—"

"Hey. Shh. First, it's Win, normally, but around here, right now, the name is Gaston."

She blinked at him. "Gaston?"

He raised a shoulder. "I liked the movie. And I use antlers in all of my decorating."

"Oh my gosh, you *are* a Marshall. That's something one of my stupid brothers—any one of the five of them would say."

He leaned back, put his arms behind his head. "What can I say? We Marshalls have to stick together."

"I gotta go. But, thanks, um, Gaston."

"You're welcome, Couz. And again, let your boyfriend know that I'm glad to make it up to him."

"Thanks." But her gaze went again to the space across the street.

Certainly, she had been seeing things. Alan Martin, double-agent, assassin and traitor did not escape, track her across the ocean only to plant himself outside an obscure coffee shop to watch her eat a croissant.

Speaking of, she wrapped it up even as she waved to Gaston and wove her way to the street.

Tried not to run back to the hotel.

Surely, dreaming. She'd just been caught up in the game she'd been playing.

With Winchester Marshall, movie star.

Maybe she was still asleep.

The elevator took a thousand years and finally she was back up on seven, headed down the hall—

The door opened just as she reached it.

York stood in the frame. He hadn't shaved, dark whiskers across his chin, and his hair was still adorably rumpled from sleep. He wore his dress pants from last night and had pulled on a tee-shirt, his phone and key card in one hand.

The other he used to grab her wrist and yank her inside.

Slammed the door behind her.

Then he pushed her against the door and kissed her. Something hard and quick and ooh, he was upset. Or, at least panicked.

Then he touched his forehead to hers and said quietly, "Where have you been?"

Oh, uh... "I...."

He leaned back, met her eyes. "I called and called only to discover—" He held up the cell phone.

Oh. Hers.

"I...went out for coffee. And croissants." She held up her grease-stained napkin. The pastry had been a little flattened in all the ruckus. "I forgot my phone."

He was breathing a little hard, those blue eyes still fixed on her. Then, he sighed and turned, walking away from her, all the way to the balcony doors.

"You okay? What's going on?" She followed him, then put her hand to his back. Tight.

"Logan called."

Logan Thorne. Their boss, director of the Caleb Group.

"And?"

York turned, and the look on his face sent a chill through her. "Alan Martin has escaped."

She blinked, and suddenly, the room shifted. Her stomach clenched and she couldn't breathe.

"RJ?" He grabbed her upper arm, and good thing because she just about toppled.

So. She wasn't going crazy.

Shoot.

She met York's eyes. "I know," she said softly. "I saw him."

CHAPTER

TWO

Y ork knew he was over-reacting. Knew that, cerebrally, RJ was fine, not kidnapped by the Russian mafia, or run over by a double-agent assassin, and she was a full-grown woman who knew how to handle herself.

Okay, *mostly*. But she did tend to get herself in over her head. Like the time she ended up in Russia, the target of an international killer, accused of murder.

Or when she followed a hunch only to be kidnapped by a traitor. That time had involved York and ended with him being thrown off a building. But he'd survived, and so had she, and he needed to just Calm. Down.

Except, "What did you say?" he said in his Very Calm Voice. It sounded more like a whisper, but whatever.

RJ stood, holding that flattened croissant in a soiled napkin, her beautiful blue eyes wide, and he could almost see that brilliant brain working, sorting it out before she answered him again.

"I...I think I saw Martin."

Yep, that's what he thought she said.

He roughed a hand across his mouth, then turned away to look out the window, to the bright blue of the Parisian sky soaring over the tops of the mansard roofs. Everything here was so...epic. From the architecture to the history...a person could get lost in the labyrinth of cobblestone streets, wandering under flower laden balconies.

At least that was his hope. Get lost, escape their life, just for a blink of time.

"York?"

"I'm thinking."

"Maybe it wasn't him. You know, I could have...I haven't had much coffee today."

He turned back to her. "Where did you see him?"

"At the coffee shop."

His eyes widened. "The hotel coffee shop?" No, no—how had Martin tracked them down—

"No. A coffee shop—café—about six blocks from here. It's... not near the hotel."

He cocked his head. "What—why?" His gaze went to the croissant, back to her.

She was wearing a pretty sundress, her hair half-dry and pulled back. No makeup, just sun-kissed cheeks. So innocent and sweet and—

"I sorta got kicked out of the hotel coffee shop, so we went to another one."

"We?"

"Oh, me and Winchester Marshall."

A beat, and he just stared at her.

She lifted a shoulder, then raised the croissant. "He bought me breakfast."

"He...what?"

"He sorta instigated the whole fiasco at a nearby coffee shop, so he offered to buy me a coffee. We found this other place, and while we were sitting outside, that's when I saw Martin."

"You went out for coffee with Winchester Marshall?" He cupped a hand behind his neck.

"It's no big deal. We're cousins, you know, so—"

"Does he know that?"

She frowned. "Of course."

He'd bet.

"He's really nice in real life. You'd like him."

Doubtful. He wasn't impressed with guys who pretended to be some sort of super spy.

"Although he did call us kissing cousins."

His eyes widened.

"Calm down. He was kidding."

York wasn't the jealous type—not really. But it was hard to compete with tall, dark and charming. "Whatever."

"Really, York. He's just a regular guy that everybody fantasizes about."

"You fantasize about him?"

"What? No. I mean—listen. Calm down. He's not on my list."

He blinked at her. "Your list?"

"You know. The list of guys I'd run away with."

"You'd run away with someone?"

"No! I...you know. Everyone has a list of people they'd, uh, well, the G-rated version is run away with. The R-rated version is—"

"I can figure it out."

"Don't you have a list?"

He opened his mouth. Closed it. "I'd never run away with anyone but you."

She smiled at him. "You are sweet."

"I'd never trust anyone else to keep you safe."

"And a little possessive."

He reached up and touched her face. "Yep." Then he leaned close and whispered, his lips against hers.

Her breath caught. Yes, that's what he liked. Surprising her. Taking her breath away. He leaned away, into her ear. "Winchester Marshall may be every girl's fantasy, but I'm the real deal sweetheart."

She laughed. And when he pulled back, her eyes were shiny. "There's no one like you, York."

He hoped that was good.

"Tell me what he looked like."

"You saw his movie posters. Tall, dark hair, blue eyes. Handsome, of course. Except he was in disguise, which is why I didn't realize it was him behind me in line. He wore a baseball cap and glasses, a hoodie and jeans—very American, but—"

Oh, for Pete's sake. "*Martin.* What did this man who you think was *Martin* look like?"

She stopped talking. Made a face. "Sorry. Close clipped brown hair, light jacket, suit pants. Sunglasses. And that scar across his forehead." She drew a line with her finger above her eyes.

He'd given Martin that scar while trying to stay alive in a speeding car in Washington state. York exhaled. "You sure you saw the scar?"

She matched his exhale. "Not sure. But...I think he was looking at me, York. I mean, I could feel it—a sort of itchy sense that he saw me. But...that sounds crazy, right? First, we were sitting sort of in the back, in a secluded area—"

He raised an eyebrow.

"I think Win didn't want to be recognized."

"Win?"

"He actually calls himself Gaston in Paris."

"Of course he does."

26

"But it's crazy right—to think that Martin would break out of jail and fly across the pond just to track us down—and how, right?"

"Track *me* down, RJ. We have history and—"

"I know. And the easiest path to you is through me."

"He wouldn't stop at hurting you to hurt me." And at that he met her eyes. "Please don't do this to me again."

"Do what?" She frowned. "I went out for coffee. And a croissant. You can't be velcroed to me, York." Stepping away from him, she set the croissant on a nearby table. "Yes, I forgot my phone, but c'mon—trust me a little." She hadn't raised her voice, but he heard it—the stubborn woman who'd followed a hunch and refused to stop looking for him even when he was lost to himself.

"I know. I just..." He sighed. "I just can't lose you, too."

Her countenance softened. "I know." Then she turned and headed to the bedroom.

What? "Where are you going?"

"To change into spy clothes." She turned at the door. "And then we're going back to the café."

Oh, he wanted to correct that—*he* was going back to the café. But her words pinged inside him. Yes, he trusted her—probably more than he'd trusted anyone. The person he *didn't* trust was Martin.

How had he found them?

And then, as he stood there, tracking back the last twenty-four hours...the selfie on the bridge. Was Martin monitoring her social media? Crazy, but York wouldn't put it past him.

Still, to be honest, it seemed far-fetched to think that Martin chased them across the ocean all the way to the 8th arrondissement.

So, probably she was safe.

Still. He returned to his room and grabbed his wallet, his

27

cell phone and dearly wished he'd brought a weapon. He did manage to pack his KA-Bar in his checked luggage, and hooked that onto his belt, but pulled his shirt over it.

Felt like overkill, really, but then again this was Alan Martin, double agent, bomber, assassin, and the mastermind of a plot that nearly derailed the American election. So, yeah, York went with the knife.

RJ was waiting for him, wearing her running shoes, a pair of jeans and a shirt, her hair slicked back into a high ponytail.

He couldn't help but grin. "Sydney, show me where you spotted our target."

She smiled back at his Alias reference. Lodged deep in her head was the idea that she was Sydney Bristow, and he liked teasing her.

Although, she sometimes took the moniker too seriously, in his mind.

He grabbed her hand, and they left the room—he left a hair in the door, and a Do Not Disturb sign on the knob.

"I'm deeply praying that it was in your head," he said. "No offense."

"None taken." She tightened her grip in his as the elevator doors opened.

They got inside, and he couldn't help but pull her against him, give her a kiss. After all, Paris.

He let her go, however, when the doors opened on the floor below and a family got in. Mom, Dad, two daughters in braids. They spoke German.

Someday maybe they'd have two daughters with braids. But the thought pinched, deep inside. Once upon a time, he'd had a son. And a wife.

He wasn't going to let Martin steal his happy ending.

They walked through the lobby, out onto the cobbled sidewalk to the smell of a nearby bistro, coffee, baked goods, the hint of flowers from the overflowing boxes from balconies above. Motorbikes passed them, weaving in and out of the traffic.

He'd scanned the area as they walked out—saw nothing, but if Martin had followed her from the café, he'd be surveying the area.

York turned onto a side street, then quickly pushed through the green doors of an Italian restaurant. He stood in the entry, peering out the window.

"What are you doing?"

"Checking for a tail."

He waited ten minutes, but no one resembling Martin passed into view, down the street or along the sidewalk.

Hmm. "Let's go."

They emerged onto the sidewalk, and he retraced his steps back to the main road.

"It's about four blocks, and then take a right, and about two more blocks," she said.

The city here spoke of history, with its Gothic architecture, the ornate roofs, the frames around the windows, the scrolled balustrades on the Juliet balconies. Amidst this, vans, cars and scooters jockeyed for space on the road, Parisians rode bicycles on the sidewalk, and he pulled RJ out of the way of a fast peddling courier.

He'd hoped to spend the day taking her to the Arc de Triomphe, making the climb to the top. And then a stroll down the Tuileries Garden to the Louvre.

Actually, he didn't care what they did. As long as they escaped their world, even for a day.

Apparently not.

"It's just up here," she said and pointed to a restaurant with an arching green awning over an eating area, that jutted into a side street. A number of bicycles lined the gated area, and even from here, it looked packed.

"Where were you sitting?"

She pulled him over to one end of the eating area, in the shadows of the building. "And Martin was standing there."

He followed her point to a park across the street.

"He was there. Just standing, staring at the café. I looked away for a second, and he just...vanished."

"Let's take a look at what he was looking at."

They crossed the street to the park. A statue of a man on a horse was littered with pigeon refuse, but pansies grew at the base, and a worn bench suggested a popular place to rest.

York stood and stared at the café.

Yes, from here, it would be difficult to make out anyone in the shadowed corner of the eating area. So, probably, he wasn't looking at RJ. But what were the odds of Alan Martin finding himself at exactly the place RJ had randomly wandered to.

With Winchester Marshall, no less.

Still, he couldn't shrug it away.

"Let's get some coffee, and see if he shows up." He crossed the street again and took a space at a vacated table.

"I'll go get coffee," RJ said. "And another croissant." She winked.

He couldn't help but smile. This might turn out to be a good day after all. She'd probably just...mis-seen. And the odds of—

His gaze fell on a man crossing the street into the park. Dark hair, shorn close, wearing a light jacket and jeans—he screamed American.

York's heart turned to a fist in his chest.

Especially when the man turned.

Everything inside York went cold. A faded, but still reddened scar across his forehead. Yeah, York had done that.

Still remembered the fight in the car that had nearly caught him in a fiery ball on the side of a mountain.

He watched as the man walked over to the bench. Sat down like he might be enjoying a lazy morning.

Stared at the coffee shop.

York's skin prickled.

Then the man opened a paper he'd held under his arm and began to read.

So, maybe it was his imagination—

"Here you go—coffee, black, and my second latte of the day."

"Sit down."

RJ frowned at him, and he kicked out her chair. "He's here."

She sank into the chair. Put the cups on the table. Glanced at the man.

"Don't look at him."

"I can't *not* look at him. My eyes have a curious mind of their own—oops!" She turned away and picked up her cup. "Sidney Bristow would not do this."

He smiled. "You need to learn the art of looking out of your periphery. Or under cover."

She turned away, looking at him, her face slightly angled. "Like this?"

"Given I can't see your eyes, oh—you're going to spill." He reached out and redirected her cup to her mouth.

She set it down. "What I'd really like to do is get some real training out in the field."

Right. Which jived so perfectly with his hope of having a home, a family.

Speaking of, he hadn't yet checked the status of his offer—

"Someone's coming." She gestured with her chin.

He glanced over. Yes, someone had approached the bench, and now sat on the opposite end. Dark skinned, immaculately attired in a pair of jeans and a button-down shirt, the man sported a trim beard and a high fade with a flat top. Middle thirties, maybe. Built.

"Is he here for Martin?"

York lifted a shoulder, directed his gaze across the street, his eyes still on the two men.

Martin put the paper on the bench. Got up.

York also hit his feet.

"What are you doing?"

"Following him."

She took another sip of her coffee, then swept it up. "Oh, fun—"

"No." He turned to her. "You're going back to the hotel."

"He picked it up."

York glanced at the bench.

The man had picked up Martin's paper.

"It's a hand-off, isn't it?" RJ dumped her cup into the trash. "Martin handed off something to that French guy."

"We need to leave it. It's not—"

"You follow Martin. I'll follow Frenchie." She was already turning away.

"RJ!" He didn't mean to raise his voice, for it to cut through the clatter of conversation, for it to sound so—sharp. Angry, even.

Or, for her to still and turn back to him, her mouth poised in that tight, grim line that—oh man, now he'd started something.

She took a step close. "Listen. I'll just follow him. And..." She lifted her cell. "I'll keep in touch. Don't you want to know what he's doing?"

He sure did.

More, he didn't want to lose Martin. If it was indeed Martin and not a creepy, eerily familiar and terribly coincidental lookalike.

Sheesh. "Fine. Be careful. Don't get close—and don't tip him off!"

"I can do this, Vaughn," she said and he rolled his eyes at her nickname, the love interest of her favorite character. "Trust me."

She grabbed his lapel, stood on her tiptoes and kissed him. A sweet peck.

And then she was gone.

It wasn't that he didn't trust her.

He didn't trust the world.

Don't get too close. Don't tip him off.

York's words ran through her head as RJ followed her mark down the street. The day had turned warm, the breezes tepid in the June heat. *Trust me.*

Frankly, she should be the one worried. Last time York and Martin met, he'd nearly succeeded in bombing the hotel where President White was celebrating his inauguration. And before that, he'd killed a CIA operative, and before that, he'd nearly killed York himself and, well, Martin's resume was too long if she didn't want to trek down the road of panic, so...

Please, York, be careful. Don't get too close. Don't tip him off.

She followed the Frenchman down a flight of stairs into the Métro. He went through a turnstile, and she had to stop at a machine and plug in her card to get a pass. The air always turned thick and musty in underground subways, reminiscent of bomb shelters, although many stations had been refaced in an Art Nouveau style. Curved brick walls were pasted with posters for upcoming shows, or fashion advertisements, with the occasional run of orange chairs or benches along the wall. At this hour, nearly noon, the station wasn't yet packed, and she spotted the man waiting on the platform for Line 9.

He looked in her direction, but she vanished behind a pillar, her heart in her throat.

Too close.

She moved away, behind the man, then pulled out her phone and texted York.

In the Metro. Taking the 9 Line.

The station began to rumble and in a moment the subway rushed in, stirring the air, whisking up dust and grime.

The Frenchman got in, and she scurried into the crowd, shuffling into the same car, through the other door. She kept her head down, hiding behind a well-dressed businessman attached to his phone via headphones.

The subway pulled out and she ventured a glance at the Frenchman.

He had the paper tucked under his arm, but now opened it and slipped something into his pocket.

She lifted her phone, pretended to take a selfie and snapped a shot of him. Then, she sent it to York. And her sister, Coco, who worked for the Caleb Group as their white hat hacker.

Can you find out who this is?

They rode for five stops, and then he got out.

She followed him, and noticed he dumped the paper in a nearby waste can.

They emerged into the fresh air to a massive square with a soaring monument of a woman, an olive branch in one hand, holding a book in the other. RJ's memory clicked in— Place de la République, to honor the French revolution.

The Frenchman crossed the square, scattering pigeons and

bypassing a few artists who'd set up stands, hoping to sell their oils or watercolors. She stopped to admire one, letting the man cross the street toward a massive, exquisite hotel, although everything in Paris was exquisite, frankly. The place boasted a beautiful courtyard with towering trees, four stories under a mansard roof, ornate balustrades at the windows and the words Crowne Plaza over the door.

She watched the man enter, and then followed.

The historical vibe ended at the door. Inside, the place had been given a contemporary face lift, with sleek desks, modern furniture, and a hip vibe. A sign near the entrance welcomed, in five languages, the attendees of the International Conference for Engineering and Technology. It featured pictures of the presenters, mostly men in beards, although one woman from Nigeria and another from Denmark were listed.

No sign of the Frenchman.

The concierge called out to her but she smiled at him, shook her head and beelined through the lobby, like she knew what she was doing.

And that's when she spotted the Frenchman boarding an elevator.

The doors closed before she could do something foolish and hop on with him.

That would have been a very un-Sydney move. Unless, of course, she put on glasses and then pretended to be a part of the conference, and maybe lost or something.

The lift dinged on the fourth floor. Stayed for a moment.

She pressed the up arrow to call it. The lift next to it opened, and a couple emerged. She scooted on and hit the fourth floor button. At the last moment, a man walked up. He wore a lanyard, and she glanced at it—ICET. Oh, from the conference. His name was in Cyrillic, but the tag, in English, said he hailed from Russia.

Please don't hit three, or two or—

He pressed the fifth floor button and the doors closed just as more conference attendees walked up. Clearly a session had let out.

Hurry, hurry.

The man smiled at her. Good looking, mid-forties, dark brown hair, drawn back behind his head in a ponytail. What she remembered of Russian men, during her brief run—nope, *escape*—through Russia, was that they were usually clean shaven, wore their hair short. So, not the usual Russian, but maybe he was here for the technology portion.

Her floor dinged and she got off. The hallway stretched a half-block it seemed, and her super sleuthing skills were clearly operating because she spotted the Frenchman at the end of the hall a moment before he slipped into a room.

She tried not to run, not to lose sight of the door, but there were so many. By the time she reached the far end, the exact door eluded her.

Now what?

Maybe he'd gotten a key to the hotel? Or probably, he was simply staying here.

Her phone buzzed and she pulled it out.

RJ guessed the time in Seattle around one a.m. but her sister often burned the midnight oil working for the Caleb group, her days spent homeschooling her son, Mikka, who was still catching up after a year of treatment for his now-in-remission Leukemia. So, she wasn't surprised when Coco responded with a, *Why?*

We spotted Martin. In Paris. He handed something off to this man.

Three dots. Then they vanished. Hmm.

She walked to the end of the hall, and when people emerged from the elevator, turned toward a door, pretending to have just walked out. She greeted them as they walked by, and then stood at the elevator. Dug out her credit card.

This could work.

Her phone vibrated.

He escaped? Really? Be careful. XO.

It wasn't like she couldn't take care of herself—and she had nothing for York's silence after her comment about getting field training.

It was almost as if he was against it.

When the light dinged, she turned and walked back down the hall, as if going to her room. A man hustled by her, and she looked over at him and smiled, playing with the card in her hand, as if it might be her key. He was tall, solidly built, with dark blond hair, glasses. Probably from some Nordic country. He gave her a tight smile, nodded, then quick walked down to the end of the hall and headed toward one of the suspected doors. Entered.

She stopped at the end of the hallway and pulled out her phone.

In the Crowne Plaza. Followed the Frenchman to his hotel room—

Nope. Deleted that last word.

Followed the Frenchman to his hotel. In the hallway outside his room, I think. Not sure what to do...

She debated, then sent it. Her other message was still undelivered.

Please, York, be safe.

For a second, she was back in a Seattle hospital watching York being arrested and dragged out by the CIA and a coldness flushed through her.

Then, she'd had no idea that she wouldn't see him for a month, and when she did, his memory would be gone. But now, like then, a darkness had seeped into her bones.

Stop, he was just fine.

Still, as she stared at her phone, the feeling poured through her.

She nearly pressed her call button, but at the moment, a door near her opened. She looked down, pretending to text, glancing up through her hair.

Frenchman came out.

And with him was the man she'd glanced at, the Viking from the north.

The Frenchman had him by the elbow, as if leading him and the Viking kept glancing at him, something drawn about his expression.

The darkness inside her took root.

She kept her head down and followed them casually down the hall, her gaze on her phone, and when they hit the elevator button, she went straight for the stairs.

And ran.

She emerged into the lobby, with no sight of them and her heart sank.

But then the elevators dinged, and she watched from behind a large fake palm as the couple headed down the hallway to a side entrance.

Then out into the street.

She took off in a run. Met the door before it could close, then watched as the Frenchman pushed his Viking captive into a waiting car—a rather nice white Mercedes, class C.

But still, they were getting away. And Mercedes or not, Frenchie didn't look like he was inviting the Viking out for dinner. Nope, she couldn't shake the idea that the poor Viking was in Serious. Trouble.

She snapped the sedan's license plate as it pulled away, toward the street.

Now what?

Oh, York would kill her. But what if this guy was in real trouble?

What if he was somehow involved in another terrorist plot against America? The last one had nearly killed their new president.

Martin was up to something, she knew it in her bones, so she stepped out onto the street.

The car had reached the end of the block, was turning right.

No—no—She shoved her phone in her back pocket and took off in a run toward the main street. See, this is why she wore her trainers, as York called them. The perils of spending his formative years in an international school where they spoke British English. He sported a hint of a British accent, even now.

She reached main street and nearly plowed over a woman walking with her pet Yorkie. "Sorry! Pardon!" She veered around them and waved her hand, hoping to alert a taxi. She'd come around to the front side of the hotel, and more than a few taxis were lined up.

But first, she turned and yes, spotted the car.

It was stopped at a light.

A yellow Volkswagen Golf pulled over, a woman with pink hair in braids at the wheel. She leaned over to the passenger side and said something in French.

Oh no. "I need you to follow—never mind. I'll tell you where to go!" She reached for the door handle.

Her hand landed on the grip of a man, behind her, who then bumped her away.

The Russian. He looked at her with a frown.

"Zis is my taxi."

"No, it's not, pal," she said and bumped him back, jerked the door.

He stood back, hands up, eying her.

"Sorry. It's an international emergency."

He raised an eyebrow and she got in. Leaned forward to the pink haired driver. Her picture and license posted on the center of the dash read Giselle.

"I need to follow someone. I don't care how far. It's important. Go—straight—it's that Mercedes at the light."

Which had turned green.

Giselle stared at her for a moment, then shrugged and pulled out into traffic.

"Don't get too close. Don't tip him off."

Giselle smiled, then shook her head. "It's like a movie, eh? Jack Powers?"

"Yes. Just like."

She leaned back in her seat. She should probably text York, tell him what she was doing. Send him the picture of the license plate.

She reached into her jeans pocket.

Empty. Oh—no—

She checked her other pockets, then her purse...

Oh, York was really going to kill her.

CHAPTER

THREE

"So, Martin had help escaping."

"Yes," Logan Thorne said on the other end of York's cellular call to D.C. Logan had picked up on the second ring, so York guessed his boss was already up, probably doing morning PT, despite the early, nearly 5 a.m. hour. "It's the only way we can account for the attack on the transfer vehicle. They knew when and where, and two of our security guys were wounded in the exchange."

York picked up his pace as Martin bled into street traffic, still not so thick that he couldn't spot him fifty yards away, but he wasn't about to lose him.

In fact, if the guy spotted him, even better.

"And twenty-four hours later, he's in Paris? Even for an ex-CIA officer, that's quick."

"Who knows how many passports and aliases he has. But how did he get on your radar?"

"RJ saw him while getting coffee—he's turning the corner, I gotta go."

"Be careful. He's dangerous," Logan said. "But don't let him get away."

"Roger." He cut off the call, then noticed that RJ had sent him a couple texts. He'd have to look at them later.

He picked up his pace, dodged a bicyclist, scooted by a magazine kiosk, and turned the corner.

Martin hadn't sped up, so maybe he didn't know he was tailed. But after a while, guys like Martin and York had a sort of sixth sense about these things, so York didn't settle into that hope.

He passed a café, the smells of lunch starting to wind out onto the street, and a number of shops, with mannequins in the windows, a shoe store. Not much car traffic here—but plenty of delivery trucks and people on scooters. He quick walked under the shadows of balconies, the scent of flowers mixing with the heat of the city, and passed a construction area, the sidewalk covered with scaffolding.

All the while, Martin stayed thirty yards ahead.

Don't get too close. Don't tip him off. His own words to RJ thrummed inside, and with it his gut tightened. He shouldn't have let her go alone. But if Martin was into something traitorous—a probably rather than a what-if—then York couldn't move his gaze off him.

But they also needed to know what he'd handed off to the Frenchman. So, yeah.

Except it rattled him, just a little, at how quickly she jumped into the potential danger. He didn't know if it was verve or naivety. But it didn't bode well for the life he'd been mapping out for them—

Martin stopped at the corner light, and turned around.

York jerked himself into an alcove entrance to a bookstore.

A woman walked out, the bell ringing at her exit and he smiled and nodded to her.

Then he fell into step behind her as she turned in Martin's direction. They passed a kiosk selling scarves and hats and York debated swiping one, but he kept going, his head down.

Please let Martin not have seen him.

The light changed and Martin crossed the street, then turned into an opening that led to an inner courtyard.

York picked up his pace, racing through the light before it turned yellow, then easing up at the entrance.

A parking lot, situated in the yard of the building. He drew up, strolling into the lot, his head on a swivel.

No Martin.

Cars packed the lot, with an area for scooters, too, and he guessed it might be an apartment building. He stood for a long minute, scouring the three entrances—big blue doors that led inside each side of the building.

Where—

The noise, a scuff behind him, an indrawn breath alerted him and he turned just in time to catch a piece of re-bar en route to his head. He slammed up his arm, deflected it—held back a grunt—and sent his fist into the face of his attacker.

Alan Martin.

The man spun back, but he was trained, and made of tougher stuff and rebounded fast with another "at bat" with his re-bar club.

This time it caught York across the ribs just as he lunged toward Martin. He tackled him around the waist and they went down in a tangle. He landed a punch in Martin's gut— the guy was lean and toned, probably from his thousand and one daily sit up routine in his cell. Martin didn't even emit a *woof.* Instead, he hooked his leg around York and rolled.

York caught his wrists just as he brought the re-bar down to pierce him through the chest.

Up close, Martin looked older, deeper lines in his face, his eyes dark, the scar York had inflicted turning a deep red. He swore and yanked the re-bar away.

York slammed his hand into Martin's chest and the man jerked off him. He scrambled to his feet, and again caught the weapon a second before Martin could run him through. This time he hung on, jerked and set his knee into Martin's gut.

The man coughed, stumbled back, the re-bar ripping from his grip. It clattered to the sidewalk and York made to scoop it up.

Martin landed on his back, pushing him into the concrete, arm around his neck. "Miss me?"

York turned his chin, got it under the man's arm, then elbowed him in the gut and cleared the hold.

York scrambled away, breathing hard.

And that's when he saw that Martin had grabbed his knife. He held it out, shaking his head. "You should have just stayed at the café, drinking your coffee. You can't stop this, York."

"I can stop *you*," York said, his eyes on the knife hand. He stepped in, meaning to grab his wrist, but Martin turned inward, elbowed him in the chin and then, heat seared his chest, right under his rib cage.

He grunted and jerked back. The knife dripped his blood from where it had sliced a line across his ribs. Breathing hard, he faced Martin, shutting down the pain from his brain.

"Try that again."

Martin grinned, blood in his teeth from York's first hit, and lunged.

This time, York side-stepped him, caught his wrist and wrenched it back. Martin released the knife but rounded and sent a punch right into York's ribs.

His knees buckled.

But his hand landed on the knife, and his grip closed around it.

He looked up, and Martin was backing away, hands up. "Just like old times, pal. You on the ground. Me...well, I did see you brought RJ along. Can't wait to catch up." He winked, even as York pushed himself off the ground. But the wound had sucked out his breath, and the world spun. He braced himself on the building as Martin took another step back.

"This is bigger than both of us, York. Stand down before you and your girl really get hurt." Then he turned and fled.

York bit back a word even as he tried to follow. But every breath seared and he slowed and again braced himself on the building.

He wanted to punch something—instead he lifted his sodden shirt. The knife had sliced to the bone, and he definitely needed stitches. But that also meant, probably, a police report and wasted time.

And of course, Martin's words about RJ thundered through his brain.

He needed to stop the bleeding, and pronto. And then find RJ. Get back to the hotel and connect with the Caleb group.

So much for his Paris proposal.

He pulled out his phone and leaned against the building. Two texts and a picture from RJ. He pulled up the picture of a man on the subway. Tried to get a fix on who he might be, but he just didn't look familiar.

The second text gave a location--*In the Crowne Plaza. Followed the Frenchman to his hotel. In the hallway outside his room, I think. Not sure what to do...*

He texted back. "Meet you back at the hotel."

The last thing he wanted was for Martin to find RJ in the hallway outside his room.

She didn't pick up the message, so he sent a call through.

After four rings, it went to voice mail. *Hey! You know what to do!*

No, actually, he didn't. Go to the Crowne Plaza or back to the hotel. But he was still bleeding and probably he needed some first aid before he ran around the city.

Hopefully she'd get his message.

He stood up and tried not to let the pain dig into his bones as he ventured back out to the street. Heading to the scarf kiosk, he bought a black patterned pashmina, and much to the grimace of the vendor, wrapped it around his chest, cinching it tight.

Keeping his head down, he tried to get a fix on his location. But he'd turned so many streets and...aw, shoot. He pulled up his phone, clicked on the map.

Nice. Over a mile away. This would be a fun walk.

Good thing the French mostly minded their own business. He also bought a hat and kept his head down as he fought his way back to the hotel. He wiped his hands before he pushed the lift button and managed not to leave a bloody trail along the golden carpet to his room.

Empty.

His heart fell a little, but she had said she'd taken the metro, so it might be a bit.

He went to his bathroom and untied the long scarf. Eased it off his wound.

The blood had dried, caked to the wound and he left fibers behind as he pulled off the scarf.

Yeah, Martin had gotten him good. A six-inch wide slice, starting just under his arm, across his rib cage, and if he'd gone any deeper, he would have punctured a lung.

He swabbed it out with water, gritting his teeth.

Where was RJ? He walked out, pressing a hotel towel—sorry—to his wound and picked up the phone. She still hadn't picked up his message, and that set a fist into his gut.

He called, but again, voice mail.

RJ, where are you?

He turned the phone to speaker, then dialed Logan.

"Do you have Martin?"

The man sounded like he'd had his first cup of coffee.

"No."

Silence.

York looked at his mug in the mirror, giving himself the expression he imagined Logan wore. "Sorry. And, I need some stitches. Or superglue—"

"Roy is headed your way. He just caught a flight from Germany. He'll be there in an hour."

"Send him to the Bristol hotel."

"I know where you are, York. I have your phone pinged."

Of course he did. "Then can you ping RJ's phone? She's not picking up."

"I'll get Coco on it. RJ sent her a picture of the man she's after. Coco is running facial recognition on him. Did Martin say anything?"

"When he cut me? Did sort of a hula dance of joy, but no big revelations. He did threaten RJ, of course. And told me to stand down."

"We're looking into his accomplices here. Could be part of the rogue CIA faction that Jackson put together. It's like rooting through an anthill—no clear players, and Jackson isn't giving up her source."

"Please tell me she's still locked up in the Metropolitan Correctional Center."

"So far. We have CCTV on her cell, and an extra guard, for now. She's complaining of her civil rights being violated, but as long as her cronies are out there—she should be grateful. I wouldn't put it past them to have her mysteriously commit suicide, right?"

"She's in a world of hurt, that's for sure." And that included her daughter, Glo, who was still struggling with her mother's betrayal. She'd dropped out of her band, the Yankee Belles, and had gone into seclusion with her husband, Tate Marshall, who just happened to be RJ's big brother. So York sort of had an inside track to the impact of Jackson's betrayal.

"I texted Coco, and she pinged RJ's phone. She's at a hotel—the Crowne Plaza."

So, maybe still watching the room. He'd head there as soon as he was patched up.

He hadn't realized he'd sighed until Logan's voice shifted, friendship in his tone. "Not the vacation you'd hoped?"

York ran a hand down his face. "Dinner was canceled last night."

"So the ring is still in your pocket?"

That's what he got for dialing Logan in on his plans. Mostly, he'd hoped that his boss would hold off any assignments during their getaway.

Like tracking down an international fugitive. Perfect.

"Listen, York. It doesn't have to be perfect. Just find a moment and spit out the question. You know she'll say yes. RJ is crazy about you."

"Call me if you get an ID on the guy she's tracking."

"Text me your room number. I'll pass it on to Roy. And York?"

"Mmm?"

"RJ will be fine. Breathe."

"Mmmhmm."

A beat. "Listen, I know Martin got away, but we'll find him."

York walked to the balcony. Could almost feel RJ's hand on his back. *I saw him.*

"Yes," York said. "I will."

They hung up and York walked out onto the balcony. Up

here, the summer winds stirred the air. He looked out into the cluttered city.

And couldn't deny the terrible clench of dread in his gut.

"Keep following, yes?" Giselle glanced over her shoulder, the eyebrow rising.

"Yes," RJ said, a glance at the meter. What if they drove all the way to Germany? She hadn't a clue how far they'd traveled in the last hour—at least fifty miles out of the city, and RJ decided she'd lost her brain when they passed Disneyland Paris, and the last McDonalds, when the landscape turned pastoral, with quaint centuries old farmhouses and scattered forest.

They'd caught up with the Mercedes while still in the city, and Giselle seemed like a pro as she settled behind a few cars, following casually, nothing to see here.

"Oh, he's going to kill me," RJ said under her breath. She was caught in the law of diminishing returns. Because the longer they went, the more she was committed to the journey.

And the more furious York would be. Not that he would yell at her—okay, maybe, but more, he'd wring himself out with worry.

Not that he didn't have reason, but...

She could take care of herself, thank you.

"Who is going to kill you?" Giselle glanced at her in the rearview mirror. "Are you in danger?"

RJ put her in her mid-twenties, pretty brown eyes, her garish pink hair pulled back into two pigtails, with bangs framing her face. She wore a black, half tee-shirt and jeans.

"No, not...really. I'm just...I lost my phone, so I can't tell my boyfriend where I'm going."

She frowned. "He sounds a little possessive."

RJ let out a laugh. "York? Um...maybe. But, he has his reasons. He lost a wife and child years ago, so he's a little protective."

"No man should tell you how to live your life." She reached into the console. "Gum?"

"No thanks. And he doesn't. In fact, I think he'd like to—but he knows better."

"That's right *sistah*." She lifted her fist for RJ to pound it.

RJ met it, smiled. "Actually, he'd have to get in line with my five brothers. They've spent their entire lives trying to tell me how to live mine—or at least how *not* to."

She leaned back in the seat, looked out the window. Waves of green fields, bordered by hedgerows and trees, the occasional stone farmhouse.

"Why?"

"Because I'm the only girl. And...I don't know. I guess I'm a little more curious than they think I should be." She looked at Giselle. "I've been accused of being impulsive. Maybe even reckless."

Giselle raised a shoulder. "All the brave things in life happen when we stop thinking and just follow our heart."

RJ wasn't exactly sure she agreed, but she nodded anyway. "I'd call York, but I lost my cell phone."

She popped her gum. "I'd let you use mine, but it's tracking the ride."

"It's okay. I'll find one when I get...wherever we're going."

Giselle leaned forward, her arms cupping the steering wheel. "Who are we following?"

"It's...actually, I don't know."

She glanced again into the rear-view, frowned. "Then?"

"Okay, so the truth is, I think he might be involved in something...bad."

And even as the words uttered from her mouth, she realized how silly she sounded. Oh boy. York was right—she was sometimes too curious for her own good. "I'm sort of, well, I work for an organization that, um—"

"Are you with the CIA?"

"Oh. No. I...nothing like that."

Giselle narrowed her eyes.

"But you are American?"

RJ nodded.

"Why are you in Paris?"

Ahead, in a valley, a Gothic church steeple rose. "I don't know. I thought it was so he could propose...but, maybe not. And now..."

"Do you want him to propose?"

She looked at Giselle. "Yes. Of course. Why?"

"It's just...you know. *He's going to kill me.* Do you want to marry a man you're afraid of?"

RJ blinked at her. "I'm not afraid of York. Ever. He...he's risked his life for me more times than I can count. He rescued me when I did something stupid in Russia, and...he'd give his life for me."

"Then...?"

"I think he wants a different life than the one we have."

Oh. She hadn't realized the truth of that until she spoke it aloud, and her words settled inside.

"What life is that?"

"Kids. A home."

"And you don't want that?"

They passed a small suburb, maybe a bedroom community of Paris, with quaint stone houses, walled off from the highway.

"It's not that I *don't* want that..." But her own voice betrayed her.

"What do you want?"

She raised a shoulder. "I guess I don't know.

Her mouth opened. Closed. "I see."

She turned off the main road and followed the Mercedes, now a quarter mile ahead, as it headed into rolling farm country.

"Perhaps are you running away from fears of being a wife and mother?"

Maybe she should run from the French way of finding her soul with their words. "Why would I be afraid of that?"

"You tell me. But you said he already had a wife. And a child. Perhaps you feel...competition?"

"No." She folded her arms. "No competition." She stared out the window. "They were murdered."

But as she thought of it, York had defied the entire world to marry Claire, the daughter of the American ambassador to Russia.

A man who later tried to kill him, so not a great choice, but still, York had given up his entire life for her. And then watched her die.

Frankly, RJ hadn't actually thought about the devastation of that until now.

No wonder he worried about her.

"So, yes, I think the idea of me following a stranger into Nowhere'sville, Paris—"

"It looks like your mark is headed to Sézanne." Giselle pointed to the village as they turned off the highway, still following the Mercedes.

"Don't get too close."

Giselle gave her a look.

They slowed and followed at a distance as the Mercedes drove through an ancient gate that led into the town.

"It's a medieval town, population about five thousand. The church of St. Denis is here."

They drove through the gate, the road bordered on either side with houses that made up a kind of keep around the central village. Not a wealthy town, most of the houses were one or two stories, with red brick around the windows and brown tiled roofs. The further in they traveled, the more Gothic the town became, with sharp black roofs and cobblestone streets. They came to a town square, with a fountain filled with flowers in the center and a massive, ancient Gothic church perched on a hill. It overlooked a large Bavarian style hotel on one side, a park on the other, and across the street, another hotel, two stories with flower boxes at each window.

The Mercedes had pulled up to the Bavarian hotel—and Giselle parked across the square, in the shadow of the church.

RJ leaned forward and watched as the Frenchman got out, then motioned the Norseman to the door of the hotel.

Giselle drummed her fingers on the steering wheel. Then looked at RJ.

"Now what?"

"Maybe I get a room there."

"Do you speak French?"

"No."

Giselle shook her head. "I think I understand your boyfriend." She picked up her phone. "If I drop you here, the fee is $258 euros. But maybe I bring you back to Paris. Free of charge?"

"No. I need to stay."

"Then you should know that isn't a hotel. It's a bar, with rooms for rent. The hotel is there." She pointed to the two story, with flower boxes. "But—"

"I'll be fine." RJ dug into her purse. Good thing she'd exchanged money yesterday, but it cleaned her out.

Giselle's mouth tightened as she took the money. "I think this is a very bad idea." She reached into her middle console and took out a card. "You call me if you need a ride. I'll come to Sézanne." She smiled. "But it will cost you."

"Thanks, Giselle," RJ said.

"I think I agree with your boyfriend."

RJ tucked her card back into her wallet and got out.

It was only after Giselle pulled away, leaving her on the cobbled sidewalk that she remembered—she'd forgotten to use Giselle's phone.

Maybe the hotel would have an office computer.

She walked in, past the fragrance of the flower boxes— pansies bursting in all colors—to the smells of freshly baked bread. To her left, the room opened up to a small restaurant, with beams running along a white-washed ceiling, and small two-person tables set for dinner.

Directly in front of her was a wooden check in desk with envelope boxes behind the desk and keys hanging from vintage hotel bobs embedded with numbers.

Oh, for cute.

A woman in her mid-fifties, maybe, with long dark hair, dressed in a simple white dress walked up to her with a greeting.

Or so RJ guessed. "I don't speak French."

An eyebrow went up, then the woman nodded and slid behind the front desk. Pulled out a worn English-to-French dictionary and pulled out a worn three-by-five card.

It read, "Welcome to the hotel Champenois. How can I help you?"

RJ slowed her speech. "Do you have any rooms?"

The woman nodded. "Single?"

Yes. "I'd like a room that faces the bar across the street." She pointed to the Bavarian hotel.

The woman nodded and pulled up her details on a laptop she stored under the desk. RJ handed over her card and debated asking to use the computer.

Or the phone.

The woman ran the card through an old-fashioned hand processor and handed it back. "I am, Juliet," she said, her words halting.

"I'm Ruby Jane," RJ said. "Thank you." She pointed to the computer. "Do you have…a hotel computer?"

Juliet nodded and gestured her away from the restaurant to a sitting room. On a table that might be as old as King Louis XVI sat a rather new flat screen computer.

"Bad Internet." Juliet pointed to an ancient, rotary phone. "Dial up."

Oh boy. "Thank you."

"Your key." Juliet handed her an actual key, as well as a piece of paper with her room number listed. 204.

"Merci," RJ said, and Juliet smiled, probably politely, but she had a warmth to her eyes.

RJ turned to the computer. She waited for the Internet to dial, listened to it connect to a modem. She logged into her gmail.

Dear York.

Don't panic. I lost my phone. But I followed the Frenchman to Sézanne, about fifty miles east of Paris. I can't be sure, but I think he kidnapped/took/met up with a scientist from a Tech and Engineering conference.

I am safe, don't worry. I'm staying at the—

She checked the address on her paper.

Hotel Relais Champenois.

Come get me.

Sorry. Love you.

RJ.

She sent it, watching the icon spin.

Then her page went blank.

Nice. She tried to log onto Facebook, to see if Coco might be online.

The screen timed out.

She got up and looked at the bar across the street.

Hmmm.

She went upstairs and found her room — a corner room that indeed overlooked the bar.

The place was quaint and simple. Beams cast down from the ceiling to the windows where a cushion tucked into an alcove. The room might be single, but it contained a double bed with a clean white comforter and a red brocade drape at the head of the bed.

The windows were open—no air conditioning here, but a ceiling fan hummed overhead, stirring the air.

She sat on the bed.

What on earth was she doing?

"Perhaps are you running away from your fears of being a wife and mother?"

Giselle's voice filtered into her head.

What? No.

But if she were honest, she'd never seen herself as a mother. A wife, maybe, but even that...

It occurred to her that maybe the reason York hadn't proposed was because he didn't see her that way.

Nothing like his one true love, the girl he'd sacrificed everything for. She'd been his wife. And had given him a child.

RJ just gave him trouble.

Maybe she was just tired, and a little stressed, and she'd let Giselle get in her head and...

She toed off her shoes and lay down, her head on the pillow, the bar still in view.

What did she think was going to happen? That she'd overhear some conversation from the Frenchman and the Viking?

Oh, this was silly, and stupid and...York had every right to be furious.

She closed her eyes and tried not to hear the voices in her head call her stupid.

Maybe it was the heat of the room, the fall of adrenaline, the whir of the fan above...

A rattle at her door made her open her eyes.

Shadows fell into the room, the sun on the backside of the day, and it took her a second to orient herself.

French village. Alone. And—

And someone was working her doorknob.

She got up, slid off the bed and crouched.

And then did the only thing her brain could conjure up. She grabbed her shoes and slid under the bed, hiding.

CHAPTER
FOUR

"Sliced with your own knife. That's gotta hurt."

York lay on the sofa and now glanced up at Roy, who was leaning over the slash across his chest, stitching it up. The guy had brought along his personal medical kit—Novocain, silk thread, scissors, even antibiotics. A regular combat medic.

"Just hurry up. I still haven't heard from RJ."

In fact, York had been ready to snag a stapler from the hotel's office when Roy showed up.

Tall, dark brown hair, darker eyes and a grim set to his mouth, Roy was a shadow, and for a few years, a ghost, his status MIA from his SEAL team. A status that really meant he'd been recruited into the clandestine services.

He had a certain set of skills that apparently included field surgery.

"You sure it was Martin?" Roy said, tying off his stitch. He reached for a tube of antibiotic cream.

York took it out of his hand and sat up. He opened the tube. "What does that mean?"

"It's just—okay, it's convenient, right, that you happened to be in the same place that Martin shows up? Like he wanted you to see him?" Roy snapped off his gloves. He wore a black tee-shirt, jeans and boots, his hair longer and curled out under a baseball cap. A grizzle on his jaw.

"Maybe." York finished applying the ointment, then reached for a bandage.

Roy ripped him off a piece of medical tape. "You probably need an oral antibiotic, too."

York taped on the bandage, one side, then the other. He grabbed a clean shirt, a white oxford and a fresh pair of jeans. Changed clothes then laced up his athletic boots. "What I need is to track down RJ and figure out what is going on." He tucked in his shirt, then picked up his phone. "Logan gave me access to the program that pings her phone. She's still at the Crowne Plaza."

He grabbed his suitcoat.

Roy packed up his kit, grinning.

"What?"

"I was just thinking about the first time I met RJ, in Prague. So in over her head but determined to warn that Russian General about the assassination attempt."

"You should have put her on a plane back to the States." He found her number and pressed send. *Please RJ.*

"Not a chance. She had this look in her eye—"

"Don't talk about that look—it keeps me awake at night. C'mon RJ!" He hung up. "Voicemail. Again."

"She really wants to be a field agent." Roy zippered his backpack. "Logan said she applied to be trained at the Farm."

York pocketed the phone, grabbed his wallet and passport, his jacket. "Yeah. When she was an analyst."

"No. Recently. She asked Logan if she could join an upcoming class."

York stilled. "How do you know this?"

Roy opened the door. "Because Logan asked if I'd train her."

York stared at him. "Train her? For what?"

"I guess whatever the Caleb Group needs her for."

Cold threaded through him. Once upon a time, he'd been the guy who did whatever was needed. And tore a gash through his soul that only a short-term amnesia and a baptism in redemption had healed.

"York, you okay?" Roy frowned.

He shook his head but pushed past Roy to the elevators. Hit the button.

"What?"

His jaw ground tight even as he pushed his hand into his pocket. The ring box sat inside like a rock. "I...I thought we had a different future. That she wanted what I want."

The lift arrived and they got in.

"What do you want?" Roy pushed the button for the ground floor.

York stared at his reflection in the mirrored walls. The years of wear on his face, a twenty-four-hour grizzle, the scar that spanned his neck. "Peace."

The doors opened and again, a crowd had gathered in the lobby, most under the age of thirty, holding signs.

"What's all this?" Roy asked as they pushed through.

"Some movie star is in town." The man's too handsome, unscarred mug stared down at them from a ten-foot poster near the door.

"The guy who plays Jack Powers?" Roy said. "The American James Bond?"

"Yep." York pushed through the door. "He's the one who got us into this mess. If I ever get my hands on him..."

60

Winchester Marshall stood at the curb, waving to his fans as he got into a limousine.

Again, the guy looked as perfect as his stupid picture. Wore a pair of jeans, a button-down oxford rolled up to the elbows, like he might actually do work, and a pair of aviators.

"You were saying?" Roy said but York turned away and stalked down the sidewalk. Whatever. It wasn't like he'd see the guy again.

Still.

His chest burned with the recent stitches, but he ignored it as they headed toward the Métro. Line 9 to the Crowne Plaza according to RJ. He followed his GPS, but kept the app that pinged her phone open, also.

He couldn't ignore the clench in his gut at her silence.

It only tightened when they arrived at the hotel. He noted a conference placard near the desk, and a lobby full of attendees breaking for lunch. He searched the crowd, but no RJ.

"She mentioned staking out his room, but the phone is pinging outside," he said.

Roy followed him outside to a street packed with taxis and Ubers.

"The ping is coming from here, but...I don't see her."

Roy was stalking the sidewalk, looking into the cars.

York followed the ping to the middle of the sidewalk, near the entrance and stared at an Uber, empty save for its driver, a younger man with short brown hair and a blue shirt.

"Excuse me." He tapped on the glass.

The driver rolled down his window.

"Have you seen an American woman. Long dark hair, wearing a pair of jeans, trainers..." He couldn't remember what color shirt.

"Is she with the conference?" He gestured to the crowd. "Too many Americans."

Right. York nodded and backed away.

Still, the ping.

A man climbed into the Uber and it pulled away. Another began to pull into its place.

"Wait!" York stepped off the curb, his gut clenching. He held up his hand as he picked up what looked like RJ's crushed cell phone. Blue case, with a pop mount in the back.

The Uber driver laid on his horn. York looked up, blinked. Stepped back onto the curb.

"Did you find something?" Roy ran toward him.

"It's RJ's." He held out the phone.

Roy took it and tried to turn it on.

York was shaking his head. He turned and searched for CCTV cameras, but nothing on this side of the building.

"Maybe you should sit down," Roy said.

And what, put his head between his knees? Yeah, he felt a little lightheaded, but nothing that wouldn't be solved by hitting something, hard.

He scrubbed his hand across his mouth. "What was she doing out here?"

"Following someone?"

That was better than abducted.

Still, he might retch.

"Let's see if anyone remembers seeing her. Do you have a picture?"

He unlocked his phone and handed it to Roy. "About a thousand."

Roy took it and opened his photos. "Be right back."

He nodded, and then as Roy headed inside, he headed down the row of taxis, repeating his question.

No one, not a one, had seen a beautiful American woman being kidnapped and thrown into a vehicle.

He stood, finally, at the end of the street, staring out into traffic, his gut tight, the smells of exhaust and heat rising around him.

Oh, RJ. What have you gotten yourself into—

"York!"

He turned at Roy's voice. He was running down the sidewalk.

"Your phone pinged—you got an email." He handed the phone to York.

Please let it not be a ransom note—

And sure, his brain didn't have to go that direction, but, there it was. He'd always be a little bit wired to fear the worst, maybe.

He opened the email.

His entire body unknotted. "It's from RJ. She's in a town east of here about an hour away. She followed the Frenchman. Apparently, he kidnapped someone."

Roy raised an eyebrow.

"I know. Maybe she does need that training. Let's hire a car."

Roy set off down the street, poking his head into taxi's. Meanwhile, York emailed her back.

Stay put. I'm coming for you.

Love you too.

Y.

He was about to pocket the phone when a text came through.

Logan.

Coco identified the Frenchman with Martin. His name is Abu Massuf, known terrorist leader with the Boko Haram. He recently kidnapped a group of Americans in Nigeria. According to Coco, he took a flight from Lagos yesterday to Paris. Not sure why. Be careful.

Perfect. RJ was on the tail of a terrorist. He should have guessed as much.

"Hey York!"

He looked up. Roy was gesturing, holding open a car door.

He jogged down the street and got in beside Roy.

"Sézanne," Roy said.

Their driver, a middle-aged, dark-skinned man, nodded.

"I hope you have cash," Roy said.

"I always have cash." York looked out the window. "Never know what trouble RJ will get us into."

Roy chuckled as they pulled away from the curb.

"I'm not exactly kidding. Her little trip to Russia ended up with us escaping on the Trans-Siberian railroad, her sister getting shot and then a showdown in Siberia with an assassin. Not to mention the fun we had in Washington state, when Martin tried to kill me."

Roy glanced at him. "So, she can keep up with you, then."

York raised an eyebrow.

"Please. It's not like you lived a tame life before you met her. We've known each other a long time, York, and that was *after* you became a spy. You've never sat down long enough to get comfortable—I don't think it's in your blood."

"It was, once."

They were driving in traffic, the clogged, dangerous streets filled with scooters and tiny Peugeots, Fiats and Mercedes, all honking. Shadows from the early afternoon sun fell from apartments with dark hip roofs, and columned renaissance buildings.

"Once. You mean when you were married and still went undercover with the Bratva?"

York pinched his mouth shut.

"Guys like us aren't meant to be married. At least not to normal girls. RJ—she's not normal, so..." Roy grinned at him.

But York looked away. Maybe not, but he sure wanted her to be.

Wanted *them* to be. Normal. Boring.

Safe.

"I put an offer in on a house in Shelly."

Silence as he glanced at Roy. The man had cocked his head at him. "Really."

"It's not a big place. It overlooks the water, lots of land...safe."

"Does RJ know this?"

"That was supposed to be a surprise for after she said yes to my proposal."

"Oh boy."

Yeah, York was starting to feel that, too.

"What made you think—"

"Because she once said she'd go anywhere, be anywhere with me and I thought—"

"And you thought that mean hearth and home in a tiny town in Washington State."

He sighed. "Eventually, maybe. I don't know. It's just..." He stared again out the window as they cut out of the city onto a highway. "It never ends."

"What never ends."

"All of it. The evil we fight. The fact that we never, really, win."

Silence.

"This Jackson thing got to you."

"Imagine if we hadn't caught her. If her assassination of White had happened and she was actually in office as the President." He shook his head. "And now, Martin..." And for some reason, his stitches began to burn. "I'm just tired."

Roy stayed silent as the tires of the Corolla buzzed against the pavement.

He glanced at the driver and wondered if he could speak English.

"Of course it never ends," Roy said finally.

York looked at him.

"It's the way of evil. It is unrelenting. And the fight is always there. Our job is to just fight the battles we're assigned to fight."

"Tell that to RJ."

"She's not the one I just spent an hour stitching up."

York drew in a breath. Fine. He turned away. "I just want to win, for once. And maybe marry the girl, too."

"You don't ask for much, then."

They were outside the city now, the landscape turning provincial, with rolling fields anchored by stone houses, sometimes dipping into a hamlet that encircled a steepled cathedral. He imagined resistance fighters hiding behind stone fences while German panzers chewed up the fields.

Funny that his imagination went there, but yes, talk about the small battles that led to great victory.

Overhead, a plane crossed the sky, on its way to Charles De Gaulle.

"Sézanne." The driver pointed to a city in the distance. A massive Gothic cathedral with a square renaissance tower rose from a hill in the center, surrounded on all sides by red-roofed stone homes. Fields encased it.

Why would the Frenchman she followed go here?

"What is this town known for?"

Roy was on his phone. "I only have one bar, but according to Google, nothing. It's old. Has a castle, and an abbey. Was rebuilt a few times. But...it's nothing."

"Sézanne. No cell. No Internet." This from the driver.

"No Internet?"

"Dark zone." He pointed to the sky.

A town with no Internet. And no cell service.

For all practical purposes, cut off from the rest of the world.

It put a hole in York's gut, and he refrained from a '*drive faster*'. But he pressed his foot on the floorboard, wishing it.

He didn't know why, but he couldn't shake it.

RJ was in trouble.

And of course, he wasn't there to save her.

She was going to die here, in a sparse hotel room in the middle of a medieval town, armed with nothing but her shoes.

And she certainly wasn't being brave about it either. She crouched behind the double bed, the late afternoon shadows cascading in through the ancient windows, stirring up the dust of travelers' past, hoping that whoever fiddled with the door handle would just Go Away.

She grabbed her shoe in a softball hold, just in case.

The door handle continued to wiggle, and then—

The lock gave.

She gasped. The door swung in.

She threw her shoe with everything inside her.

"Hein!" A man ducked away, just as the shoe zipped past him.

She half expected it to be the Frenchman who'd she'd followed to Sézanne, a tall black man who'd kidnapped the poor Norwegian scientist.

Or even Martin, doubling back for her after he'd taken out York—

She cut that thought away. Nope.

Instead, an elderly white man, dressed in overalls and a jaunty beret, sporting a trimmed white beard stood in the frame, clutching a toolbox and staring at her with widened eyes.

"Oh. Sorry. I..." She scrambled over the bed, holding her other shoe. "What are you doing breaking into my room?"

He let out a barrage of French, turning away from her and now gesturing to someone in the hallway.

Juliet appeared, putting her hands on the man's shoulders, and landing her own barrage of French. She pointed down the hall and the man lumbered away.

Um...

Juliet turned to her. "Oh, désolée! Excuse, Excuse." She pointed at the door number, shook her head. "Mauvaise chambre."

To her best guess, the man had entered the wrong room.

RJ held up her hand. "It's okay." She offered a smile, even as Juliet picked up her not-so-lethal shoe. She handed it back to her.

"Désolée."

"It's fine," RJ said. "Really."

But...she pressed a hand to her stomach. "Food?"

"Ah. C'est fermé." Juliet shook her head.

Right. "Okay, thank you."

Juliet backed out of the room, still apologizing.

RJ moved to the window and stared out at the bar and grill across the street. An ancient building, it looked like it had been plucked out of Bavaria, with stucco between waddle and daub framing, a false thatched roof and cute window boxes that hung off skinny Juliet balconies.

If she wasn't alone, having run off by herself, following her stupid impulses, this might be romantic.

Sorry, York. How she wished she had her phone. York was probably losing his mind. Hopefully he'd gotten her email.

The street was quiet, a few cars parked in the cobblestone square under the shadow of the church. The air was rich with the scent of meat roasting and she guessed it came from the bar.

Her stomach suggested she go over, but—

The Frenchman stepped out of the building. She leaned away from the window, but she watched as he pulled out a cigarette and lit it.

Then he walked down the street, away from the bar.

Away from the man he kidnapped.

She watched him go, then stepped back to her window and stared across the street. Where are you, Hans?

There. A light in the far window, second from the end.

Maybe.

She glanced in the direction of the Frenchman. As she watched, he got into the passenger side of a non-descript gray van. Looked like an Amazon delivery truck, if they had those here.

The truck drove away.

Slipping on her shoes, she grabbed her key, locked her door and headed down the stairs, out into the street.

Looked both ways—and in moments she was inside the bar.

She'd stepped back in time. A giant stone hearth anchored the far wall, the wall behind a long wooden bar was stacked full of bottles of spirits. Another floor to ceiling rack held wine.

And from the kitchen behind the bar lifted the redolence of a hearty lunch. Pot roast. Potatoes. Yum.

A man looked up from where he was cleaning an empty round table. He pushed in a red leather chair and looked up.

"Bonjour." She lifted her hand in greeting.

He nodded at her.

She glanced at the stairs. "My friend is upstairs..." Oh, wow, she was a bad liar. She just hoped in the dim light he couldn't see her face burn.

Instead, she turned and fled for the stairs. They creaked as she ascended, and on the second floor, a green padded carpet led to the end, with dark mahogany doors on each side. The floor creaked in pain as she headed down it, but she stalked to the last door, the one facing her building, and took a breath.

What. On Earth. Was she. *Doing?*

But in that moment, she couldn't erase from her mind the look on the man's face as he'd walked out with the Frenchman.

If he was in trouble, she was here to help.

No matter what York, or her brothers, felt about it. Frankly, she'd been the one to first uncover Jackson's treason, so she deserved a little faith, thank you.

She knocked.

Movement sounded on the other side, and she stepped back and braced herself.

The door unlocked and opened.

In front of her stood the man from the Crowne Plaza, the Viking, with the blond hair and drawn expression.

"Hello," she said softly, then looked down the hallway.

No Frenchman.

"Can I come in?" Yes, warning bells were sounding, along with York's voice, but given the way the man stared at her, his blue eyes wide, a little shock in them, he was more afraid of her. Sure, he was tall—easily over six feet, handsome in a short-haircut Thor sort of way, but also nerdy because he wore wire rimmed glasses, which he now pushed up his nose as he nodded.

She stepped inside, then turned and closed the door.

Locked it.

Then she turned back to him. "My name is RJ. I...I saw you get kidnapped in Paris."

The room was small - just a single bed, a side table, dresser, a small closet. On a luggage stand sat an old boxy suitcase. A door to an adjoining room was ajar. The place smelled old, musty, tinged with cleaning oil.

The man sank onto the small bed. It creaked under his weight.

"You were kidnapped, right?"

He glanced past her, to the door, then back.

"I'm...I think I can help you."

He swallowed. Shook his head.

"What's your name?"

He took a breath. "Mads. Fischer."

"Hello Mads. Can I sit down?" She gestured to a nearby straight chair, and he nodded. "Why were you taken? And who is the man who took you?"

He exhaled and clutched his hands to his knees. Swallowed.

"Do you speak English?"

"Yes."

"Then?"

"I'm a scientist. I am not a terrorist. I do not want trouble."

Terrorist? "I...I don't want trouble either. Are you in trouble?"

He swallowed, then nodded. "My wife...was murdered."

Oh.

"They said she jumped, but no. She would not—she would—not!" His eyes filled.

"Who is your wife?"

"Anja. Anja Fischer." He looked away. She put him in his mid-thirties.

"I'm so sorry about your wife, Mads. Why do you think she was murdered?"

He met her gaze, something fierce, suddenly, in it. "She wouldn't leave Hana."

She gentled her voice. "Who is Hana?"

"Our daughter."

"Your daughter. In...Norway?"

"Germany."

"Is she...safe?" He pursed his lips together. Shook his head. "I did not know. I didn't know!"

She touched his hand, but he jerked away. Got up. "You must leave. If they find out—"

Holding her hands up, she rose. "Okay. Okay. But who is *They*? What do they want?"

He ground his jaw. Shook his head.

"Mads, I want to help you. I work for an organization that... well, we can help."

He stared at her, drew in a breath. Shook his head.

"Listen. I'm not alone here. I can get help. We can keep you safe. And Hana."

Her words felt right, deep in her gut.

Mads stared at her. Then, he nodded.

"Yes. Good. Should we get you out of here?"

He got up, still nodding. Then, "Not without the Marx device."

The Marx device? He reached for the suitcase.

Oh. The Device. Whatever was in that suitcase. He picked it up but as he turned, he glanced out the window.

Stilled.

"What?"

He pulled back. "Nein." He set the device down.

"What? What does that mean?"

He turned to her, his hands out. "Raus!" Then started to push her toward the door. "Go, go away!"

"What? Is he coming back? The Frenchman?"

Mads nodded, and she pushed him back, and ran to the window.

The gray delivery truck was parked in the square. She

leaned against the glass and just barely spotted the Frenchman as he entered the restaurant.

Oh. Stink.

One stairway. One hallway, and if she didn't move fast, he'd know—

She headed toward the door.

Just as she turned the handle, the hall creaked.

She let go of the handle.

Turned.

Not under the bed, and there was no adjoining bathroom.

Mads stared at her, his eyes wide. "You will get us killed."

Not today.

She stalked to the window and opened it. Just a Juliet balcony, and not a real one at that, but bars that jutted from the window, a decoration. And from it, the overflowing flower boxes.

Better a broken leg than a bullet through the head.

For Pete's sake, York was really going to kill her.

She put her leg over the edge. The balcony wasn't wide enough for her body, but she managed to wedge her leg down into the space, then heave her other leg out, letting it dangle over the side.

"Close the window after me."

He was already shutting it.

She leaned away from the window, her wedged leg securing her to the building.

But she looked ridiculous, a part of the greenery, overflowing out of the balcony. Please don't let the Frenchman see her.

Worse, the ground was further than she'd imagined.

A car drove by. She looked away, a little horrified at herself.

Inside the room, the door opened, and now she heard French, and not for the first time wished she'd paid attention in college. But no, she'd focused on honing her Russian, thanks to her foster sister.

In her next life, the one she lived after she dropped to her death in a backwater French hamlet, she would learn French.

And, maybe parkour.

Hey—that was it. The next window wasn't so far away—maybe four feet—and if she could swing herself out, she could grab the bars, climb onto that, and then let herself out through the next room.

She leaned out, trying to grab it, but it was still over a foot away.

Fine. She hooked her knee over the edge and tried again. Closer, but still a good eight inches.

But if she pushed off with her lower foot, and released her hold with her leg—

Yeah, and if she missed, she'd fall to her death.

But maybe she simply hooked her upper foot into the bars, and still pushed off with her lower leg and then if she fell, she'd just end up upside down.

Which would be ever so perfect.

Oh, next time she suggested she go off alone, she hoped York would remind her that she wasn't Sydney Bristow. Not even close.

Steps inside, and she heard shouting.

This couldn't be good.

She eyed the balcony. Eight inches. She could do this.

Grabbing the railing, she moved her upper leg around the bars and wedged it into the rails, so she was balancing on the edge, holding on with her hands.

Then, taking a breath, she turned, hooked her foot into the bars.

Please don't die. Please don't—

She jumped.

Her heart stopped, her breath caught as she stretched for the other balcony.

Her fingers touched steel. She gave herself another push—

Her foot dislodged but she closed her hands around the bars.

Then, slid.

Hang on!

She reached the bottom of the balcony, jerked and her body fell hard. The fall woofed out her breath, but she clung to the bars, dangling.

Don't look down. Don't—

But the weight of her body cut into her hands, loosening them.

She grunted, swinging her foot up, trying to land it on the wall, but it slipped off. Worse, the movement jerked her grip and one hand broke free.

She swung away from her perch, her grip burning.

No—*no*—

It broke free.

And then, she was falling.

CHAPTER
FIVE

See, this was why York should put a GPS tracker on the woman he loved.

Not that he would, but if he did, then he wouldn't show up in a town and see said woman trying to do a Spiderman along the face of a building.

As it were, he had nearly missed her as they drove into Sézanne. Their taxi driver pulled up to the hotel RJ had named in her email, and York had gotten out of the car and made for the front door.

If Roy hadn't called out his name, stopping him, then pointed to the spectacle of RJ leaping from one balcony to the other, some twenty-feet off the ground—

And if York hadn't simply followed his instincts and taken off across the street she would have left an ugly splat on the sidewalk, probably taking out a planter of geraniums.

As it were—

"Gotcha."

He wasn't trying to be cute—it was more of a statement of

relief, even fury, the spill over of watching her dangle, then slip off the balcony.

The fear he wouldn't reach her in time.

He pulled her against him, breathing hard from his dash across the street.

For a second, she just stared at him, also breathing hard, those blue eyes blinking in disbelief. Then, "York?"

"It's not Superman."

Then she threw her arms around him, holding so tight she might cut off his breathing. "You're here."

"I'm here." He let her legs down, then put his arms around her, holding her back. She could probably feel his heart pounding, trying to leave his body.

She leaned away from him, her hands on his shoulders. "How did you find me?"

"Why are you climbing out of a window?"

He looked up. The drop wouldn't have killed her, but she might have broken something. It was simply the memory of her acrobatics that stole his breath, cinched his chest.

She, too, looked up and caught her breath.

"There is an explanation, right?" This from Roy, who'd followed him across the street.

RJ looked at him, then back to York and took his hand. "Let's go."

The fact that she might have been sneaking out of a hotel room had stirred in his head, but it didn't take root until they were across the street, her glancing over her shoulder, as if checking for a tail.

Then she practically pushed him into the foyer of the hotel. Roy followed them in.

A woman stood at the counter—pretty, in her early fifties, maybe, with dark hair. He nodded at her, but RJ hadn't slowed down and now dragged him up a flight of stairs and down the hall.

She pulled out a key on a wooden fob and opened the door. Stood at the opening, holding her hand out.

He went inside, followed by Roy.

The room was small, quaint, and built for one, with a small bed. The ceilings sloped down to a dormer window.

Which gave a head-on view of the hotel across the street.

"Your Frenchman is in that hotel?" He gestured with his head.

She nodded. "And the man he kidnapped, a German scientist named Mads Fischer."

York lowered himself onto the bed. "I'm afraid to know how you know that, but start at the beginning. I'm bracing myself."

Roy folded his arms and leaned against the wall, his mouth a tight line.

"Did you get my email?"

He nodded. "Did you get mine?"

She shook her head.

Right. Not that it would have made any difference, probably.

"How did you end up hanging off a balcony?"

"It was the only place to go when the Frenchman came back. Mads was terrified—he thinks the man killed his wife."

He'd mentioned starting from the beginning, right? York sighed, then ran his hands over his face. Why couldn't he just have a nice, romantic vacation in Paris, where he proposed to the woman he loved?

"Listen, I didn't mean to get in over my head. I was just...I just followed my instincts. They said Mads was in trouble, so I followed him here, and...I was right." She crouched in front of

York. "He has a device—he called it the Marx device—and wouldn't leave without it. We need to figure out what it is."

He glanced at Roy. "We need to get a hold of Logan."

"What is his wife's name?"

"Anya. Fischer."

York looked at Roy, who pushed away from the wall. "I'll see if I can use their phone."

He left the room. York drew in a breath.

"Are you mad?"

Mad? Maybe. Scared, yes. "No. I was just...you can't do this, RJ. You can't just go...disappear. I was out of my mind."

Her face twitched, and for a second, he expected an argument, a defense. Maybe even, a *you're not the boss of me*—

"I'm sorry. I know."

He blinked at her.

"I realized that while I was hanging off that balcony. I just...I don't know why I listen to my impulses rather than my brain."

"You have a very effective brain. One that was trained by the CIA to figure out problems. But you're not Jack Powers, right?"

She nodded, and then pressed her hands to his chest.

He winced. Aw, he didn't mean to, but all the exertion of running across the street, then catching her—he might have even ripped a stitch or two.

She recoiled, frowned, and he looked down to see if any blood had broken through.

"Are you hurt?"

"I—"

Her fingers unbuttoned his shirt, and she opened it, stared at the bandage across his chest, her mouth opening. "What. Happened?"

So, maybe he had a story to tell too. "Martin. We had…um… a little tussle."

"A little—*tussle?*" She had peeled back the tape to see the wound, reddened, and yes, a little bloody. It didn't look like any stitches had pulled out—Roy's excellent handiwork. But it wasn't pretty. "This isn't a *tussle*—he could have killed you!"

He took her wrists and moved her hands away. Then he re-sealed the tape. "I'm fine."

She sat back. Blinked, her breaths falling over each other.

Silence fell between them.

"You can't expect from me what you won't expect from yourself," she said. "I don't want to lose you, either."

His mouth twitched. "It's hardly the same thing. I spent years training, learning how to defend myself."

"It doesn't matter!" She got up. Shook her head. Then stalked to the window. Wiped her hand across her cheek.

"It *does* matter," he said, something igniting inside him. "It matters because I can handle myself. I don't go jumping off balconies or following men who could kill me!"

Okay, maybe scratch that last one.

But maybe she didn't notice because she rounded on him. "We don't know anything about that Frenchman. Maybe… maybe Mads is over-reacting—"

"His name is Abu Mussaf. He is a *warlord* with the Boko Haram. From Nigeria. And he recently kidnapped a group of Americans. So yeah, I think there should be some big over-reacting here."

"Oh." She folded her arms. Swallowed. "Well. Okay." But she stared at him for a long beat. "Then even more reason for us to find out why he was meeting with Martin, and why he took Mads."

"No!"

He didn't know where the volume came from. But in his

mind's eye, he was running a scenario where Abu found her in that hotel room, and...

She recoiled at his word.

Now he was mad. He got up. "Enough of this. We did our job—now it's time for us to leave and let Roy take over—"

"Are you kidding me? Martin is out there! And now this Abu guy has kidnapped, even killed a woman, and we don't know why. The last thing we should do is pack up and go home!"

"You are so stubborn."

"Yeah, well if I wasn't, you'd still be sitting in a backwoods town in Washington State going by the name Mack and serving French fries to the locals." Her eyes flashed.

He said nothing. Because she was right.

Her finding him had triggered his memory. Brought him back to himself.

Except, "Maybe I would rather be Mack Jones. Maybe I want that life, a family, a home—no international drama, no stitches, no moments where I watch the woman I love dangling out of a hotel window, about to drop to her death."

"Now who's over-reacting?"

He stared at her. Shook his head. "This is it, isn't it? This is the life you want. Always looking for trouble, living on the edge—"

"Don't you?"

He took a breath. "No. No I don't."

Silence fell between them. And it was now or never, maybe.

"That's why we're in Paris. I wanted to propose."

Her mouth opened. "I thought, after...well, that maybe you didn't want to get married again."

He reached into his pocket and pulled out the ring box. Opened it.

It wasn't supposed to go down like this, and now he'd wrecked it. But he needed to know.

"Yes, or no?"

She swallowed, her eyes wide. "You haven't asked me a question."

"I've been asking you this question for a year and a half. But, here goes. Will you marry me, RJ?"

Her chest rose and fell, then she put her hand over her mouth, and tears filled her eyes.

What? Was that a yes? Or a no. "I don't under—"

"Of course I will."

Her words coursed through him like a flame.

Yes. He reached for the ring.

She put her hand over it. "But I need to know...what does this mean for us?"

He raised an eyebrow. "What do you mean?"

"Have you not been paying attention to our conversation? I mean that...what's next? Because right now we have a situation across the street that we can't walk away from."

"We can."

"I can't."

He closed his eyes.

The warmth of her palms touched his face. Her voice gentled. "You once told me that you'd go anywhere, as long as it was with me."

He had said that. Roughly a year and a half ago. But that was then...Now...

He opened his eyes. "I still will, RJ. But...don't you want a normal life? A home, a family?"

Her hands slid from his face, her eyes meeting his. "I do. Of course I do, but...I also know that...I just want something bigger. Something that makes an impact. Can't we have both?"

He ignored the ache of her words, pocketed the ring, and

instead put his arm around her waist, pulling her close. He didn't know how. But right now, "Yes."

Then he lowered his mouth to hers and kissed her. Her lips were soft, accepting, and she responded with all the passion and life that was the woman he loved.

Just being with her made the world drop away. The past, crazy, twenty-four hours, the rush of panic, the confusion lodged in his chest.

Desire sparked deep inside, swept through him. She was hope. Healing.

Home.

And when her arms laced around his neck, he simply stopped thinking.

Oh, how he loved her. And once upon a time, he had said he'd follow her anywhere.

He would. And maybe they could figure it out.

Of *course* they could figure it out.

She made a soft noise, and it only turned to flame everything inside. It didn't help that her hair twined through his fingers, her soft body molded to his.

Not yet. He pulled away, very, too aware, of what he wanted and touched his forehead to hers. "I love you."

"I love you, too," she said softly. She leaned away and met his eyes. "Yes, I'll marry you."

So maybe this wasn't such a bad proposal after all.

He was reaching for the ring when the door opened behind them.

Roy came into the room and York stepped away.

He got a side-eye from Roy. "It's not like I don't know what you were doing."

RJ smiled, but turned away.

Roy shut the door. "I got a hold of Logan, and he ran a search on Anja Fischer. Her body washed up in the Seine yesterday evening."

York stilled. RJ whirled around. "What? You don't think she was that woman we saw last night?"

His brain was going there too.

"She was attending the Tech conference in Paris and went missing two days ago. Her husband was also at the conference, and according to sources, he is also missing."

"Mads," RJ said.

"She and her husband are both physicists. They have a daughter."

"Hana."

"Yes. She's currently undergoing cancer treatments at the Hope Children's Cancer Center in Heidelberg, Germany."

"And her parents were both at a conference? In Paris?" York shook his head. "I don't buy it."

"According to Logan's research, Anja holds a patent on a high voltage capacitor, and Mads has one on a vector inversion generator."

York just looked at him.

"It's a device that's used to generate a high-powered electromagnetic pulse. One that could be directed."

"Or targeted," RJ said.

York frowned at her.

"In other words, it could be used as an EMP weapon, to take out electronic devices." She turned back toward the window. "Mads had what he called the Marx device. It suddenly makes sense. In 1924, Erwin Marx created an electrical circuit designed to create a high-voltage pulse from a low-voltage DC supply. Mads must have improved it." She looked at him, then Roy. "A device like this, with enough power, could generate enough pulse to take out anything with a circuit board."

"Like a computer?"

"Or a phone, or anything that uses a computer to run." She looked out the window. Across the darkening sky, a plane left a plume of white. "What we have to do is get inside that hotel room and find out what they're up to." She turned to him. "We need to plant a bug."

He wanted to close his eyes, shake his head, but the fact was, she was right.

And he had only one choice. Help her.

Because he certainly couldn't walk away.

York let go of the velvet box.

Now he really wanted to go home. But one look at RJ said, Not A Chance.

And really, what could he say, because right then, words from his conversation with Roy in the car rose in his head. "Fight the battles we're assigned to fight."

And now, finally, he knew what he was really doing in Paris.

She felt like a bona fide spy sitting beside York, watching him craft a listening device. He had sort of morphed right in front of her eyes to the man she'd first met in Russia—an aura of sexy intrigue about him as he disassembled the devices he'd purchased at a local electronics store. Another stop at a hardware store had scored him a soldering iron and wires.

On the tiny desk in her room, the casings of a stereo amplified listener and a wireless FM transmitter lay empty after he'd taken out the boards from each.

He had deft hands, precise, practiced. Watching him work did something to her insides, and all she could think was...

Yes. A thousand times yes, she would marry him. Finally.

Except, after Roy burst into the room, York hadn't taken out the ring box again. It still sat in his pocket and she felt a little weird asking for it.

But then they'd shifted right into spy mode, and something had sort of lit to flame inside her. This is who they were—RJ and York, Super Duo.

Except his question sat inside her. *Don't you want a normal life? A home, a family?*

Of course she did.

Someday.

Maybe.

Or maybe she wanted both. Like she said—something bigger. Something that had impact.

Something that mattered.

She glanced at York. He was finishing his soldering, his mouth in a grim line, and she could almost hear his words. *This is it, isn't it? This is the life you want. Always looking for trouble, living on the edge—*

"Don't you?"

"No. No I don't."

But here he was, jumping right back in. "What are you doing now?"

"I'm disconnecting the wires from the boards, and then from each microphone. I need to extend all of them about six inches."

She watched, then glanced outside. Night was falling, the sky bruised over the red roofs of the village.

Roy had left to do surveillance on the building.

Probably also grabbing a bite to eat. What she wouldn't give for one of those baguettes she spotted at the hotel restaurant when they'd returned from shopping.

Maybe after they'd run their op.

Their op. She smiled.

He glanced up at her. "What are you grinning about?"

"Just...nothing. What are you doing now?"

"I'm also extending the wires for the power sources."

A tiny puff of smoke lifted from where he soldered the wires into place.

"How does this work?"

"The two microphones of the amplified listener will pick up the sound, which will be sent through the FM transmitter. That will send the sound over a specified FM frequency." He handed her a small transistor radio. "Find us an unused frequency."

She picked it up, then walked to the window. Heard the question she'd spoken to Mads, *"Who is they? What do they want?"*

"Did you find a frequency?"

Holding the radio to her ear, she ran the dial until she found clear fuzz on the line. "87.5"

"Great." He tuned his transmitter to the same frequency. "Testing—RJ can you hear me?"

"I'm standing right here."

He shot her a look. "Go into the hallway."

She took the radio outside, into the hallway.

"RJ, have I told you how much you drive me crazy? Or how much I love you?"

She smiled. Opened the door. "I heard you."

He was standing in the window, holding the device. With the sun fading, against the dim light of the room, he was a shadow, with wide shoulders, lean hips, an outline of confidence and she could feel the burn of his gaze in her bones. "C'mere." He said it softly, into the mic.

She walked over to him.

He reached out and pulled her to himself. Set his mouth

against her ear. His breath tracked down her neck, and her insides sparked.

Oh, yes, she was marrying this man.

"Stay here," he whispered.

She put her hands to his chest and forgot his wound as she pushed away. He grunted.

"Oh! Sorry—but, seriously? York—I've been in the hotel. I know my way around."

"Yeah, and last time you were in there, you nearly landed on your head, trying to escape." He had pulled back but kept his voice low.

Low and lethal.

Oh, she knew him when he got this way.

"I'm going with you."

"Not on your—"

The door opened behind them. "Abu is on the move. He left here on foot. I don't know how long you have." Roy, breathing hard. "You need to do this, now." He bent over, grabbed his knees. "They had to pick a town without cell service."

York nodded, and started to step past her, but she grabbed his hand. "Not without me."

He turned, his mouth pinched. "Fine."

Then he grabbed a book on the desk. "Where did you get that?"

"The nightstand."

She turned the spine her direction. "A Gideon Bible?"

"No. An edition of Dante's Inferno I found downstairs. I just pulled the cover off the Bible."

"Why?"

He opened the lid. Inside, he'd carved out the pages and set the listening device. "We'll plant it in the bedside table."

"I can't believe you defaced a Bible."

"Just the cover. Not the pages." He headed for the door.

She was hot on his tail.

Roy was already downstairs and was pulling out a chair at the restaurant, clearly his perch for watching the bar across the street.

RJ handed him the radio.

Then she caught up to York, who was crossing the street.

He glanced at her. His mouth a grim line. "Fine. Do everything I say."

"Bossy much?"

He shot her a look.

"I promise."

He took her hand, the book in the other.

They walked into the bar. A few patrons sat at tables, and she spotted the man she'd seen earlier behind the bar, pulling a beer. A few candles were lit in the fireplace, the night clearly too warm for a fire, but it added to the ambiance.

"Upstairs," she said.

He nodded and she followed him up the stairs.

A couple came down the hallway, and he kept his head down, walking toward the room second from the end.

She pushed him past it, to the end. "Here. Abu is in the adjoining room."

"You know this, how?"

"When I was in Mads room, the door was open."

He nodded, and then paused outside the room. Handing her the book, he pulled a toolkit from his pocket.

"Where did you get that?"

"Roy. Shh."

He glanced at the lock, selected his tools, and then inserted a tension pick and a rake into the keyhole.

"I want you to teach me how to do that."

He glanced at her. "Not today."

"Someday."

His breath drew in.

And then, the lock released. He opened it and pressed her inside.

The room was identical to Mads'—spare, with a single bed, dresser, small closet, a duffel bag on the luggage cart—only now the door to Mads' room was closed.

And a laptop sat on the desk.

Oh, she wanted to grab it.

"No nightstand," she said.

"Put the book in the dresser and let's go."

She opened the top drawer. Empty. She put the book inside.

Outside, in the hall, the wood creaked.

Her eyes widened even as York crossed the room, grabbed her, and slipped into the closet.

Small, very small, and he had to duck to not hit his head on the rod. She tucked in with him, and he braced his hand over her shoulder and pulled the door mostly closed.

"Shh." His warning was barely heard, just a breath beside her, and frankly, her heartbeat drowned out most of it, the way it slammed inside her.

But oh, hiding with him, his body pressed against hers in the soft darkness sent a thrill through her. And he smelled good, too, musky, manly and her rebellious mind went to the kiss in the hotel room, right before Roy walked in.

Oh, this man could steal her breath out of her body, her thoughts from her mind. She turned her face into his, found his ear. "Is it Abu?"

He shook his head.

In a moment, the door closed again.

York leaned up and eased the closet door open.

On the desk was a tray, the dishes covered with a towel. The smell almost made her leap for it.

"Let's get out of here before he comes back," York ground out. He took her hand and headed for the door.

Took a breath.

Opened it. She half expected Abu to be standing in the hallway.

Nope. York practically yanked her out of the room, quick walking down the hall.

Steps on the stairway made him halt.

He turned, his eyes wide and then pushed her against the wall. Braced his hands on either side of her.

And kissed her.

Oh.

Oh!

She wrapped her arms around him and dove in, kissing him back, putting umph into it, as if they were honeymooners who'd forgot themselves on the way to their room.

The steps hit the landing, and York put his arm around her, pulled her tight and deepened his kiss.

She simply hung on, lost in the fantasy. Or maybe this was their real life—it could be. Should be.

The steps slowed, then hurried down the hall. The door opened.

She opened her eyes and glanced in her periphery.

The Frenchman disappeared into his room.

York let her go, met her eyes, his fierce.

She smiled.

"Don't." He took her hand again and headed down the stairs.

"Don't what?"

He said nothing, all the way until they were outside, then pulled her around to face him. Shoulders rising and falling, he said nothing.

"C'mon, York. Loosen up. We were fine."

"I don't think I get that loose."

But then, he smiled. Something small, something that also lit his beautiful blue eyes. "Oh boy," he said and shook his head.

"I'm hungry." She pointed to the restaurant. "Are you hungry?"

"I think I've lost my appetite." But he grinned.

She pulled him across the street. See, they were going to be just fine.

CHAPTER
SIX

York hadn't dreamed of her in over a year, maybe two.

Hadn't found himself walking into a dank, oily warehouse, the tinny smell of blood in the air, only to find Claire bound, beaten, and hanging from a beam.

Hadn't relived the moment when he took her down, when he broke, right there in the shadows, his wife's beautiful eyes glassy, unseeing.

But as York sank into the dream, he tasted it again. The horror. The fury.

The helplessness.

Her blood turned his shirt sticky against his skin, his hands slippery. He pulled her to himself, and heard the cry bubble out of him, almost feral.

And then he rocked her. Just rocked her, weeping in his sleep.

Just like he had Lucas, when he found his baby son in the bathtub, alone in death.

No—

But the memory contained no mercy and he now held

sweet Lucas, with his chubby thighs and wet smile, gray in his arms.

He groaned, ragged edged and so loud that it yanked him free.

No, not free.

Never free.

I'm sorry, Claire.

York opened his eyes and stared at the plaster ceiling, the moonlight casting across the room. Sighed, and sat up, running his hands over his face.

She was still right there, in the fragments of his fading dream.

"I wasn't sure if I should come over there and wake you or not."

He glanced over at the voice.

Roy, sitting in the chair, listening to the radio with an ear piece. "You were shouting."

York said nothing.

"Nightmare, or memory?"

York pushed off the sheet—it was tangled and sweaty anyway—and reached for his pants. "Both." He shucked them on. "Anything from our friend across the street?"

"Nothing. He ate dinner, drank some wine, checked on his captive, said his evening prayers, then went to bed."

"A boring terrorist, then."

"Just living the dream."

York walked over and stood at the window. The same view as RJ's room, next door.

With everything inside him, he wanted to knock on her door, pull her into his arms, close his eyes and dream the last twenty-four hours away.

"The last time I was in Paris, I eloped with my wife, Claire."

Silence. Then, "So this was what—a do over?"

"A fresh start."

"Did you do it, then?"

He glanced back at Roy and raised an eyebrow.

The man leaned back in the chair, his legs crossed. "Propose."

York nodded. "And she said yes."

"So, then—?"

"So, it's complicated."

Roy said nothing. York turned back to the window.

"Claire was murdered. And, we had a son. He was also murdered."

Silence, then. "I know. It was in your dossier."

Hmm. He should have guessed that Roy would have read it. He'd probably vetted York when he'd joined the Caleb group.

"It was my fault. I was made by the Bratva, and they...sent a message."

"How old was your son?"

"Eight months."

"The file said you found your wife."

York nodded. Drew in a breath. "My prayer is that she died before they hung her."

He closed his eyes.

"The final step in peace is forgiving yourself."

York opened his eyes. "The hardest step."

Roy made a noise of agreement.

"She loves this life."

A beat. Then, "We're back to RJ."

"You should have seen her tonight. We had to hide in a closet, and...it's like a game to her."

"That's because she has you to keep her safe."

He glanced at York over his shoulder. "I don't know. I lost my memory and disappeared a couple years ago, and she was relentless in finding me."

"I know."

"She could do it."

"Be a field agent?"

He nodded. "And right down to my bones, I hate that thought."

No, not just hated...she scared him. But she also thrilled him because yes, as they'd hid in that closet, her huddled next to him, all their old moments rushed over him.

All the old moments where she fit into his clandestine life and made it brighter. From the moment he'd saved her from an assassination attempt in Moscow, to helping track down Damien Gustof, the man who had killed York's girlfriend Tasha, and frankly, maybe even Claire and Lucas.

All those moments that told him that together, they were better.

But maybe she wasn't safer. Not with him in her life.

Because Roy's words sort of hit him. York *would* always be there to save her.

And maybe she counted on that too much.

"In my worst nightmares—again—someone from this life shows up and kills the woman I love. And it's even worse if she's running hard into trouble."

"You do have your hands full."

Once upon a time, the same could have been said for her. He'd been the one who chased the bullets. But then she'd entered his life, and everything had changed.

He thought it was because he'd found his happy ending, or at least the hope of it.

"How can I love her and not say yes to her dreams?"

Silence from Roy.

He turned.

"Don't ask me. I keep it uncomplicated."

Yes, for all York knew, Roy had no one in his life. No one but the Caleb team, and even then, Roy was mostly a ghost.

"I just thought...I don't know. That I could walk away from all this. But what if I'm lying to myself? When I lost my memory, I lived with a man who brought me to church. Not to get weird, but I found faith. I found forgiveness. And I've tried to hang onto that since then, but...sometimes..."

"Sometimes you wake up in the middle of the night in a sweaty ball of fear and horror?"

Spoken, weirdly, like a man who understood.

York lifted a shoulder. "I told her once that my life wasn't conducive to a happy ending. That I wasn't a good person. She sort of made me believe that things could be different. That I could start over. But as much as I've tried to change, or prove otherwise..."

"She still wants her James Bond."

He let out a huff. "Or Jack Powers." He shook his head at the memory of the wanna-be hero.

Roy smiled. "Right. All I know is that you can't force her to be the woman you want. You can only choose who you want to be."

"Thanks, Dr. Phil."

"Hamilton Jones. He told me that once upon a time, back when I was a tadpole."

"During BUD/S training."

"Had a girl who followed me to BUD/S. I hoped she wanted the life I wanted...didn't work out."

Didn't work out.

Yeah, that wasn't going to happen to him and RJ. Not if he had a say in it. York walked over to the bed and pulled on his tee-shirt. Then he slipped on his shoes. "I need some air."

"Don't take too long. It's nearly your shift."

He lifted his chin to Roy, then stepped out into the shadowed hall.

The floor creaked as he tiptoed by RJ's door, and he nearly stopped, thinking of the way she'd kissed him in the hallway.

He could figure this out.

He *would* figure this out.

The cool air of the night pressed through him as he stepped onto the street. He walked to the center of the square and sat on the cement edge of a fountain, mostly dry. A beheaded saint stood in statue above him, holding his head.

Huh. He sorta felt like that most of the time—his head, his common sense severed from his actions.

Because if he were honest, really honest...

For a moment in that closet, the past rushed over him.

He'd liked being 007. Liked the way she looked at him, as if he were really James Bond.

As if he really could save the day.

So maybe the fight wasn't between the life he wanted and the life she wanted.

Maybe it was that deep inside he'd been lying to himself.

Did he really think he'd be happy flipping burgers in a small town in Washington state?

He glanced at the window—Mads'—then the one where they'd set the bug. Where a terrorist slept. Or stared at the ceiling, hatching up destruction. Chaos.

Evil.

It never ends.

Maybe, but he had to get off the carousel. Find footing. Peace.

Because then, maybe, finally, he could wake up from the nightmare.

Of all the places for a terrorist to hole up and develop his sinister plot, it had to be in a place without decent internet.

RJ sat back in the office chair down in the lobby of the hotel watching the cursor spin. Really, they could have gone back to Paris, run her Google search and returned in the time she'd put together her spotty dossier on the Marx device.

She'd spent most of the day at the computer while Roy and York listened for any tidbit of information spilling from the room across the street.

Now, she was crabby, and her stomach burned with the smells from the kitchen of the hotel, winding out into the room. The restaurant had set out tables on the sidewalk with jaunty umbrellas, and she spotted Roy and York sitting at one of them, York with a glass of wine in his hand, Roy with a frothy beer, his earpiece connected to the transistor, nothing to see here. They ate a fresh baguette, dipping it on olive oil in a bowl on the table.

The entire thing looked so exotic and European and...York, that she simply couldn't stop looking at him. He wore a pair of jeans, boots and an oxford, the sleeves rolled up at the elbows, his jacket hung over the back of his chair. He hadn't shaved, so a fine layer of dark whiskers with hints of gold layered his chin, and under the fading sunlight, his hair had turned a deep bronze.

He laughed at something Roy said, smiling, and her entire body turned to liquid. For a moment, she was back in the hallway last night as he kissed her, so much confidence, power—no, possession—in his touch.

Her York. And yesterday, when they'd sneaked into Abu's

room to plant the bug felt dangerously close to the life she'd dreamed for them.

Adventure. Intrigue.

Purpose.

Maybe he felt it too, because he'd been strangely quiet today. Could be frustration at the lack of actionable intel from the bug. But it felt like something more. Something deeper, stirring inside him.

Her web page finally loaded and she read through the specs. A report from the military—thank you top level security clearance—about the likelihood of an EMP bomb attack, and the measures taken to protect sensitive areas, like bases and nuclear reactors.

Yes, her brain went there, because if Martin was still in league with Russia—and a rogue Russian faction that wanted nothing more than a war with America, or at least the threat of it—then an attack on American soil seemed probable. Yes, her mind was reaching, but she'd done her research.

An EMP bomb took out anything run by a computer. Which, in America, meant just about everything.

It sent goose flesh up her arm.

What they needed was to pull Abu Massuf and Mads Fischer into custody and ask some hard questions. But not without Logan's permission, and maybe a few more able bodies, although York and Roy could probably handle the grab.

And now she was thinking like a spy, and it was exactly this line of thought that made York think she didn't want to settle down.

Raise a family. Make casseroles, drive kids to soccer practice, attend band concerts, and host the annual fourth of July party.

Someday. But not yet.

And she simply would ignore the way the thought put a fist into her gut. What was her problem?

She copied down some specs from the report, then logged out of her portal in the Caleb Group.

Then she headed outside.

The heat of the day had subsided leaving behind a glorious evening. The hues of the setting sun streaked across the sky in layers of deep orange, lavender and crimson. The church bells were ringing, echoing across the square. York rose as she walked over to their table and pulled out a chair. "How goes the research?"

"Without knowing what kind of device it is, it's hard to know what they might be targeting, if that's even their goal." She put her notebook on the table. "Basically, an EMP bomb causes shock waves that sends out a powerful electric pulse that takes out anything with a circuit board—like I said, anything with a computer. Medical equipment, vehicles, laptops, phones, weaponry—even our hydro-dams are controlled by computers."

"That's fantastic," York said and reached for his wine.

"I thought EMPs were huge. I saw Ocean's Eleven." Roy said. He wore sunglasses, and stared out into the square, his dark hair curly behind his ears, rocking the tourist vibe. Sorta. Because anyone who really looked at him would see the former SEAL in the way he surveyed the cars, the people who walked home from work carrying their groceries.

He was either a very dangerous, or very safe, man.

Depended on what side you were on.

"It depends on the radius," RJ said as Juliet came over. "Can I have a glass of what he's having?" She indicated to the deep red of York's wine.

"Cab Franc," he said. "It's great with the bread."

She tore off a piece in the basket. "An atomic bomb is the

largest, of course, but you can have even handheld EMPs. It depends on the capacitor —or how the energy is stored. The bigger the capacitor, the bigger the pulse, the bigger the range. The technology has been developed to target their pulse via the Marx generators. I looked into Anja's patent and her capacitor can hold ten times the electrical energy of a capacitor of the same size." She dipped the bread in the oil.

Yum.

York handed her his glass and she washed it down with the wine. She didn't know why, but the gesture felt very romantic.

So maybe they were fine.

York took the glass back. "Which means they can hide a potentially very potent bomb in something the size of a suit-case. Point it in the right direction and disable anything."

"And they're sitting across the street," Roy said quietly. "I'm not sure why Logan is sitting on this. We should be in there, grabbing everything."

"Agreed," York said. "But Abu is dangerous, and I don't know about you, but I walked into France without a weapon."

"We can fix that," Roy said.

Yes, dangerous.

Juliet returned with a glass of Franc and another basket of bread. "Dinner?"

RJ picked up a menu. All French.

Roy spoke up, and rattled off a number of items from the menu. When she walked away, he turned to them. "I got some *foie gras* and lamb chops."

Silence fell between them, and she looked at York, the way he was studying his wine glass. "Not the Paris vacation you'd hoped," she said.

A smile lifted up one side of his mouth. He looked at her. "Turnips."

Heat spilled through her, and she met his eyes, the memory

of his words stirring inside her. Once upon a time, he'd said, *"I'd have turnips if it meant you were with me."*

York took her hand.

"Maybe I'll take supper in my room," Roy said.

"Maybe that's a good idea," York said.

"York. Stop. Roy—sit down." She looked at York who smiled.

"Roy. Where are you really from?" She barely knew the guy—just that he always seemed to show up exactly when they needed him. And then disappeared just as quickly.

"Originally? I was born in San Diego. But my dad was in the Navy, so we moved around. My mom finally got tired of it and settled in Florida. My Dad came and went out of Pensacola."

"He was a SEAL, like you, right?"

He stilled. "How'd you know?"

"Ham told us when we were in D.C. Said you were on his team, back in Afghanistan."

Roy's lips pursed, and he nodded. "That's a story." He took a drink of his beer, and the silence after it said he wasn't telling it.

But she knew it—the story of the ambush of Hamilton Jones' SEAL Team, the capture of Roy and Logan, the rescue mission that got Ham kicked out of the Navy. He'd started his own global Search and Rescue team, along with a private security company, so he'd floated to the top of that disaster, but it was still a wound.

As for Roy, since he'd been reported as MIA, after the rescue, he bled into the shadows, an asset for the CIA until even that had gone south.

Now, he worked for the Caleb Group. She didn't know exactly what he did. Probably for the best.

He still showed up, and that's what counted.

Juliet brought their appetizer, pâté and thin sliced croquettes.

RJ was spreading the pâté onto her bread when, across the street, the same van she'd seen earlier pulled up to the hotel. "York—that's the van. The one Abu left in."

It was getting dark, the lights of the restaurant flickering on, candles lit at the tables, so she couldn't make out anyone getting in the van. But in a moment, it pulled away.

"We should follow it," Roy said.

"With what?" York said.

But Roy got up and disappeared around the building.

In a moment, RJ saw him drive away on a scooter.

She sat back and looked at York. "Did he just steal a scooter?"

"I hope he doesn't expect me to save any of this for him."

She shook her head. "Should we follow him?"

"He can take care of himself."

"You seem very unconcerned about the fact that there could be a—" She lowered her voice. "Bomb across the street."

He leaned in. "I am. What is there to bomb here, and why?" He spread the pâté on a croquette. "Let's just sit tight and watch. See how this plays out. My gut says we're at the beginning of this thing."

He popped the bread into his mouth. "Yeah, this is good." Wiping his mouth with his napkin, he leaned back, crossed a leg over another and lifted his glass. "At least we got the French dinner I hoped for."

Yeah. And sitting here with him... "Um. So, about that ring."

He raised an eyebrow. "You meant it?"

"What?"

"Your yes?"

"Absolutely."

He pulled the ring box out of his jacket and opened it.

Gorgeous. White gold, with a massive diamond in the center with tiny diamonds cradling it. "York. It's...it's beautiful."

He smiled. Then, even as he looked at her, he frowned, his gaze casting off her, toward—

The bar. Or no, the rooms over the bar.

And in the room not quite at the end, flickering as if—

The explosion blew out the window, and took out the umbrellas, toppling the tables, the chairs, the pâté.

York leaped on her, and in seconds, she was on the ground, his body over hers.

Screams, the roar of a fire, shouting. York rolled off her, grabbing her even as he got up.

Flames burst out of the windows from Mads' room.

"Mads!"

She started for the pub but York yanked her back. "Not on your life!"

"But he could be in there!"

"He's dead!"

"No—no—Look!" The window of the room next to Mads had been flung open. A man hung out the window.

"It's Mads!"

She untangled herself from York and ran across the street. The flames burned against the twilight, turning the street to fire. Sirens sounded in the distance.

"The fire department is on the way! It'll be okay, Mads!" She waved her hands below.

"I'm locked in!" He was coughing, the smoke from the adjacent room filtering into his window. The ancient cement walls might hold off the flames, but the roof was an inferno, and just might cave in on him if they didn't get him out.

"York, we gotta go get him!"

"Have you lost your mind?" His grip on her arms tightened. "That roof is going to cave in."

"They're not going to get here in time. C'mon—I know where it is!"

She started for the door, but his arm hooked around her, pulled her back. He rounded on her.

The look in his eyes scared her a little. "Stay. Here. I'll get him." He turned toward the door, then rounded back. "Don't you dare follow me."

Oh.

And then he was gone.

"Down the hall on the right, not the last door!" Aw it didn't matter, he was gone.

She backed up. "Help is on the way! He's coming, Mads!"

Mads had backed away from the window, had even shut it, the smoke too thick to breathe.

York, please don't die.

She stepped back, her hands over her mouth as one of the neighbors showed up with a garden hose and began to spray the building.

The flames had engulfed one end of the house, were climbing down the wall.

Behind her, the crowd shouted. The pub had emptied, and she spotted the owner. He was staring at his pub, his face wrecked.

Hurry, York!

The sirens turned deafening, and in a moment, the firetrucks arrived—two of them. One with a hook and ladder, another with a hose and tank. They assaulted the house with water. The mist fell over RJ.

They were taking too long.

She should go in.

The door opened.

Mads came charging out, coughing, a wet towel over his head.

She caught him, even as he went to his knees. "Over here! We need help!" She gestured to an ambulance that had pulled up.

Then she turned toward the door. York?

And right then, screams lifted as the entire end of the pub collapsed in a terrible spray of spark and flame.

"York!" Her scream drowned inside the roar of the fire, the shouts of the firemen. She sprinted toward the door, but this time it was Mads who took her arm. "Nein!"

She jerked her arm out of his grip, but he grabbed her other arm.

"He's in there—!"

"RJ!"

She whirled around at the sound of her name, and spotted York running down the sidewalk from the far side of the building, opposite the damaged section.

His face betrayed the soot of the fire, sweat ran down his face, and his shirt sodden.

And under his arm was tucked a laptop.

She took off, and nearly bowled him over, her arms around him as she buried her face into his neck.

"I thought—"

"I know. I know." He was breathing hard, and then began to cough. She let him go, and he leaned over, still emptying his lungs.

"Do you need oxygen?"

He shook his head, stayed down a moment, then stood up. His eyes watered, red-rimmed from the smoke. "I'm okay—I just need a second. But look what I grabbed." He held out the laptop.

She took it. "Whose is it?"

"Dunno. It was in the room with your scientist."

Mads had run up to them. "We go now. We go!"

She looked at him. His skin also bore the hue of fire, his eyes reddened. But the way he kept looking up the street...

Yes, maybe.

"C'mon," she said and pulled them across the street. Juliet was standing on the sidewalk, and she frowned as she led them inside and upstairs.

Her room was quickly becoming spy central.

She closed the door behind them. York sank onto the bed, still coughing.

"What happened?"

She looked from York to Mads and back.

Mads walked to the window, his gaze on the still blazing building. "We have big problem."

CHAPTER
SEVEN

N ow they were really in it.

York couldn't ignore the pit in his gut as Mads explained the fire. Or maybe it wasn't Mads' explanation of the Marx device and how it had overheated and sparked the fire.

Maybe it was the drawn expression on RJ's face, the way her gaze kept flitting over to him.

Yes, he might have momentarily panicked when the roof came down behind him as he fled the hotel. Might have, in that moment, wished he was back in Shelly, flipping burgers, a baseball game on the flatscreens, listening to their local crooner, Raven, playing out on the patio. And occasionally looking at the door, waiting for RJ to come in, sit at the long wooden bar of Jethro's and update him on her latest research.

So maybe they never really escaped the clandestine work of the Caleb Group.

But honestly, he was tired of running into every fire that ignited.

Now, he stood at the window, aching for a shower,

watching for Roy's return. Behind him, RJ was pacing the room, sorting through Mads' story.

"So, you're saying that Abu is building a replica of your device?"

"Yes, but much bigger."

That was what York was afraid of. "Where?" He turned away from the window, probably already knowing the answer.

"I don't know. Nearby."

"Why here? In Sézanne?" RJ, too, looked worn out, her hair falling out of her ponytail, her eyes reddened.

Probably he'd never forget the way she shouted his name, ran toward him, threw herself at him.

Yeah, he knew that look, knew how it felt. His chest still hurt, not just from her grip, or from the coughing, but his wound had really started to ache.

He needed sleep. A vacation from his vacation.

"Because no cell tower. No Internet. Nothing to surge."

"In case the device malfunctioned?" York said.

He nodded. "Here, we are invisible to the world."

Something— "Wait. Have you been here before?" York asked.

Mads nodded. "There is a lab in a farmhouse. I don't know where—they always blindfolded us."

"Us?"

He swallowed, looked away. York put him in his mid-forties, maybe. Dark blond hair, good looking, maybe. Sturdy frame. Sort of a Bruce Banner type.

"Anja. And me." He pushed the frame of his glasses up his nose. "We also worked with a Russian. A man named Ruslan. He was at the conference also."

"Why the conference when your daughter is in the hospital?" RJ asked.

Mads' mouth opened. Closed. "It was the only way."

"The only way for what?" York folded his arms and leaned against the wall. What he really wanted was to find himself horizontal, but he had a feeling sleep was hours away.

"The only way to pay for Hana's treatment," he said softly. Then he took off his glasses and ran his thumb and forefinger across his eyes. "I have made a grave mistake."

"Why?"

"Because it works!"

"What works?"

"My prototype!" He looked up.

RJ held up her hand. "Calm down. What do you mean? Your room just exploded."

He sighed as if they might be imbeciles. "I did that on purpose. So they couldn't duplicate my device. But it is too late."

York gave him a side-eye. "I don't understand."

"Ruslan has my drawings, my design. They wanted my prototype to compare it to theirs...and now, with Anja's capacitors, I fear it is ready."

"Ready?" A chill brushed through York at the word. "For what?"

"I do not know." He put his hands on his head. "But it is my pride—my pride. I should have created a defect. Instead, I built a creation that..."

His silence dug into York.

RJ knelt in front of him. "That what?"

He looked up. "With Anja's capacitors, there is no telling how great the impact of the pulse will be."

"The EMP pulse."

"Yes."

"What makes your device so special, Mads?" York said. "People have been building EMP bombs—"

"It is not a bomb! It is a...a weapon. Targets chosen."

"What kind of targets?" York moved to stand in front of him. "Military bases?"

"Nuclear reactors."

A beat. "What?" RJ said.

"The cooling rods of nuclear plants are controlled by computerized systems. They will disable them and then..." He made a poofing gesture with his hands.

"No. The computer systems in nuclear plants are behind Faraday cages for this very reason," RJ said.

"Not the ones on submarines. Or battleships. Or Aircraft carriers. Or cruise missiles."

"We don't have nuclear powered missiles," RJ said quietly.

"Russia does," York said. He drew in a breath and walked to the window. "What does Alan Martin have to do with a bomb that could disable a Russian nuclear missile?"

Too much silence.

RJ got up. "We're tired. Maybe we're over-thinking this."

"I should have killed Martin."

He stared out the window.

Overhead, a plane appeared in the sky, its lights pinpricks against the velvety darkness, heading away from Paris, east towards Switzerland.

He'd like to head toward Switzerland, take RJ with him, maybe forget the last twenty-four hours. But frankly, maybe he wasn't the guy who could walk away either.

Shoot.

Then, as York watched, the lights of the aircraft simply blinked...off.

He blinked, leaned into the window. What—?

Unlatching it, he opened it and leaned out.

Nothing. As if the plane had simply...vanished.

Huh.

Maybe he'd imagined the plane. Maybe he'd seen a satellite. Still...

"We need to go back to Paris," RJ said quietly, coming up behind him. "I can't decrypt that computer without Coco's help, which means I need the Internet."

He nodded, still searching the sky. Weird.

"My daughter needs me. I must return to Germany," Mads said.

"We'll hire a car in the morning," RJ said. "You can come back with us."

"I will secure a room for the night," he said. Behind York, the door clicked shut.

"Do you think it's safe for him to be away from us?" RJ asked.

"You might ask if it's safe for us to be with him."

RJ's arms went around his waist, her head against his back. He tucked his hand over hers.

"You scared me," she whispered.

"Mmmhmm."

He turned and pulled her into his arms. Lifted her chin. "Now you know how it feels being around you."

Her mouth tightened. "I've always known how it feels, York. If you remember, you killed a man right in front of me, on the train in Russia."

Oh. Right.

"Maybe you're right. Maybe..."

"What? We go home?"

She met his eyes. "You really scared me when you didn't come out."

"I know."

Her hands pressed his chest, traced the outline of his bandage.

"Maybe we finish this, and then...retire to that house you want to buy."

He blinked at her. "Really?"

"I don't know. Is that even an option for us?"

He made a face, then touched hers. "It depends on the people we want to be."

She met his eyes. Then, she put her arms around his neck and brought his lips to hers.

Oh, she tasted good. A hint of wine still on her tongue. He put his arms around her, pulled her against him as he leaned on the wall, and kissed her back.

Wow, he could forget himself. Forget where they were, forget his best intentions, forget that they weren't officially married yet.

In fact, as she deepened her kiss, in his head he was scooping her up, carrying her over to the skinny bed and losing himself in the life he wanted.

RJ.

She tore him in half—part of her beckoned him into a life that he saw when he sat on the deck of his rental house over-looking the lake in Shelly. The other part tugged him into the man he had been, the one who, as she put it, had a larger purpose. The one that just couldn't walk away.

Or maybe it was just the only life he knew. Maybe he was a fool to let himself believe in anything else.

"I want to be your person." He felt her hand in his jacket pocket, and she drew away, holding the velvet box. "So?"

He reached for it. Met her eyes. "So—?"

The door opened.

He was really going to strangle Roy. "Seriously? Knock!"

Roy stepped in, breathing hard. "I...hate...this...town." He stood up. "They set it off."

It took a beat, then, "The EMP?"

And there went the final thread of hope that Mads was overreacting, that they hadn't walked into an international plot, that the world wasn't in peril, again.

York closed the ring box, slipped it back into his pocket. And wanted to hit something.

"Yes. I followed them out of town to an empty field, in the middle of nowhere. They pulled off and then...I don't know. There was a hum, like a machine firing up. And then something terrible happened. There was a plane flying overhead. I watched it from Paris. Not a big plane—maybe a private jet. It was almost directly overhead, and then...nothing. Lights blinked off."

"I saw that too," York said. He stepped away from RJ. "I thought I was seeing things."

He ran the back of his hand over his mouth. "No. It was there and then...it crashed. I watched it go down. It exploded. The freakin' plane exploded."

York just stared at him.

"It took out a *plane*?" RJ said. She turned to the window.

York followed her. Sure enough, in the distance, a faint glow edged the darkness.

"Oh..." RJ said. She put her hand up to brace herself.

"Where is the van now?"

"I lost it. It took off back for town, but I ran out of gas."

"How did you get back?"

"I ran until a car picked me up. Let me off outside of town."

That accounted for the sweat, the smell.

"Perfect."

"I got the make and model. But we need to rope in the Caleb Group. See what they have on Abu and his accomplice."

"Accomplice?"

"He got out of the driver's side to smoke a cigarette. I

couldn't see him well in the darkness, but solid, maybe six foot plus. Had a ponytail."

"I saw a guy like that at the conference in Paris," RJ said, turning. "He tried to steal my cab."

Aw. See he was doing just fine and then she had to say something like that. His gut clenched.

"We can't wait until morning, RJ. We need to get back to Paris now."

Roy nodded.

"Can you find us a car?"

"We don't have to steal one. I got us a ride." RJ pulled Giselle's card from her pocket and gave it to Roy.

"I'll use the hotel phone." Roy left them.

York turned to RJ. "Let's get Mads."

She stopped him with a hand to his arm. "When this is over, I want that ring on my finger."

He stilled, then pulled out the box. Opened it. Pulled out the ring.

Then he got down on one knee. "Just to make it official."

She smiled. "Yes. Just to make it official." Then she held out her hand.

He fitted the ring on her finger. She held it up. "Pretty."

He just about said something cheesy. Instead, he stood up, backed her against the wall, and braced his hand over her shoulder, and kissed her.

She clung to him.

It was almost as if everything would turn out okay.

He finally pushed away from her. Took a breath. "To be continued."

She smiled, and it lit inside him, kept him alive as he headed downstairs.

Mads wasn't in the lobby. The counter was dark.

He rang the bell on the desk, but no one answered. A sign on the counter, in French suggested they were off duty.

So, then, where was Mads?

He walked out onto the sidewalk. Outside, the fire in the pub had died, just the stink of creosote and burned wiring in the soggy air. Firemen were mopping up. A crowd remained, despite the late hour.

A quick scan suggested no tall German scientist.

"Giselle is on her way." Roy, behind him.

"Did you find Mads?" RJ asked, coming out of the hotel.

He shook his head.

She took a breath. "I think I know what happened to the guys in the gray van." She held up a pair of wire rimmed glasses.

Oh no.

"Where did you find those?"

"In the lobby, on the floor."

In the lobby, where it was dark, and no one could see him abducted, again.

York walked over to RJ and took her hand. "Don't get any bright ideas."

All she could think was that York must be more hurt than he let on for him to still be sleeping.

RJ shot a look at the closed bedroom door of the suite, then turned back to her chat with Coco. Sure, her eyes were gritty, her bones soggy, but she couldn't scrape from her mind the fact that Mads was in trouble.

No, the *world* was in trouble, if her tired mind was right, and the rabbit trails of terror her imagination had taken as they rode back to Paris with Giselle. Roy talked with her in French the entire ride home, as he sat beside her in the front seat. Meanwhile, RJ's brain played out all manner of dire circumstances.

Military ships attacked.

Planes taken down.

Communications destroyed.

Emergency services cut off.

The entire electrical net in the US shut down.

Chaos, looting, panic.

And not to mention the whole Nuclear Meltdown scenario.

Her brain hurt. Maybe she should shut herself away in her room and get some shut eye, too.

Outside, the sun had risen, casting a glorious beam over the dark mansard rooftops of Paris. She'd caught some sleep in the car when her brain had finally powered down, her head puddled on York's lap in the backseat.

But it was still evening in Seattle when they arrived at the hotel, so she'd gotten online with Coco and started their hack into the computer's security system.

Oh, how she loved high speed internet. Coco had control of the laptop and was working her hacker magic. It helped that she'd worked both sides of the hacking equation when she lived in Russia.

RJ>>How's it going?

COCO>> Still running the program. Sit tight. How are you?

RJ>> Tired. But York finally proposed.

Coco>> !! When's the wedding?

When the world is safe?

RJ>> One thing at a time.

Coco>> Girl. York is the One Thing. And it's TIME.

She laughed.

RJ>> When I know, you'll be the first I tell.

Coco>> I wouldn't be upset if you eloped in Paris. Just sayin'.

Huh. Maybe.

She got up and headed over to the coffee bar, poured herself a cup of joe, then walked to the window.

No news yet of the plane crash, which felt strange, but like Roy said, it was a smaller plane. Maybe the French news service simply hadn't posted it yet.

The door to the suite opened and she turned—no, jumped, really—and spotted Roy entering.

He looked at her and raised a bag seasoned with grease spots. "Croissants."

"You're my hero."

He grinned. Really, he was a handsome man. Strange that he didn't have a girlfriend. Or maybe he did. Who knew, with Roy, what life he lived?

Clearly not one that involved a home overlooking a lake, a barbeque, a couple kids.

The thought hit her even as she walked over to the counter, where he'd put down the bag.

Or maybe he did. Maybe he simply separated his life that well.

She reached into the bag and pulled out a chocolate filled croissant and a napkin. Roy had retrieved his own and walked over to the computer.

"Still not in yet."

"Nope." She walked over to the sofa and sat down. Fought the urge to put her feet up, lay down, close her eyes—

Except the minute she did, she'd find herself standing outside on the sidewalk watching the building collapse. Hearing herself scream.

She played with the ring on her finger.

Yeah, maybe York was right. Enough of this life. What was

she thinking, really, that she could be a super spy? Her last attempt had nearly ended up with her as a splat on the sidewalk.

"So, he did it, huh?"

She looked over at Roy. He sat on a chair, his feet on the coffee table.

"What?"

"Proposed."

She held up the ring.

"That took some guts."

"Hardly. I've been in love with him since he saved my life in Russia."

"There's no doubt he loves you. But he's got a trail of pain that...well, I'm not sure what would happen if he lost you, too."

"He's not going to lose me."

Roy raised an eyebrow. "Says the woman that—"

"Stop." She held up her hand. "I can be impulsive. I know this. But I've learned my lesson. I'm not going anywhere without York."

He didn't blink, or move his gaze off her.

"What?"

"I've seen you, RJ. I've seen you when you figure something out. You can't sit still. You have to do something."

She swallowed, looked away.

"Tell me that you aren't itching to find out where that scientist went to."

Her gaze returned to him. "Of course I am. He has a daughter who needs him. But I'm not going to hop a plane to Germany, or...wherever. I know who I am. And who I'm not."

"What are you not?"

Her throat thickened. "I'm not a superspy."

He smiled, one side of his mouth. "Sure you're not."

"What does that mean?"

"Just...you tell yourself that enough, you might believe it."

She frowned at him. "I can't defend myself in a fist fight, I can't shake a tail, I can't hotwire a car—"

"I can teach you all those things."

She stilled. "What?"

"Logan asked me if I would teach you spycraft. Our own version of The Farm. Only, real life." He took a sip of his coffee.

"You would do that?"

He nodded, then gestured with his chin. "But not with that on your finger."

She held up her hand. "My ring?"

"York."

She stared at him. "You want me to give up *York*? What kind of friend are you?"

"The kind that knows what it would cost him. And, frankly, you."

"That's not fair."

"I thought you already made your choice."

She drew in a breath. "Maybe I have."

He raised an eyebrow as she got up and returned to the computer. Sat down. "You'd better hope that York doesn't find out about our conversation."

A smile creased his face. "He'd agree with me."

Oh.

Jerk.

She turned to the computer.

RJ>> How's it going?

Coco>> Nearly there. I did some searching online. You can't legally get married in Paris unless you live there for forty days. Italy might work, but I'd suggest Switzerland or Czech Republic. Prague—so gorgeous!

RJ>> Coco—

Coco>> We're in!

The screen splashed open. RJ watched as Coco took control of the cursor. Her video appeared on the screen.

Her dark hair had grown out, no longer purple and she wore it up in a ponytail. Behind her, the kitchen light glowed, and she wore an oversized Blue Ox hockey jersey, courtesy of her hockey goalie husband. "Hey sis."

"Hey," RJ said, aware of how tired she must look.

"Oh, hey Roy."

RJ turned. Roy leaned over her shoulder. Lifted his coffee. "Coco."

"Let's see what we have here." She opened his email. "Um, who did you say this computer belonged to?"

"I thought it was Abu Massuf," RJ said.

"This is all in Cyrillic. Unless Abu is Russian..." She clicked on an email.

RJ could read it as well as Coco. "Ruslan Gustov."

"Who is Ruslan Gustov?" Roy took a sip of his coffee.

"Let's find out." Coco opened another screen and pulled up a Google search.

A picture appeared in images. Long dark brown hair, high cheekbones, Slavic features. It nudged a familiarity deep inside her.

Yes. "I saw that man at the conference. He was the man who tried to take my taxi!"

Coco had opened another page, this one in Cyrillic, a news report from 2001 of a Russian science award. A much younger Ruslan held up a ribbon with a medal on the end. She put him at maybe sixteen. And beside him, his arm over his shoulder, a grinning much older sibling.

RJ stilled, and behind her, Roy made dark noise.

"That can't be right," Coco said.

RJ looked at Roy. "No."

Roy took a breath and stood up. "Was this planned? For

York to be here, for you to see Martin, to pull you both into this...whatever this is? Or maybe Martin stalked you. But how would he know where you are?" He ran a hand over his mouth. "What if this was a ploy—the handoff in plain sight, to draw you in."

"Gustov is a common Russian name." But Coco's voice betrayed her own dubiousness. "It's like Johnson, or Smith or Nelson—"

"It's the same man!" Roy winced, cut his voice down. "Sorry."

In truth, RJ had never seen Roy rattled.

Ever.

"Are you sure?" Coco said.

"I'm sure," RJ answered. "I'll never forget what Damien Gustov looks like. In life, and in death."

"He is dead, right?" Roy asked. "I wasn't there."

"Very dead. He landed on a rebar pole. Skewered through. I promise, the assassin known as Damien Gustov is dead."

"But his brother isn't," Coco said. "And somehow, he's part of this mess."

Roy finished off his coffee, then crushed his cup and dropped it in the waste-bin. "We can't tell York."

RJ shot him a look. "What? No. I can't lie to him."

"You want to be a spy? You need to learn how to keep secrets. And if York finds out that the brother of Damien Gustov knows who you are, that you 'accidentally',"—he finger quoted the word, "ran into him. Nope, he'll lose his mind. Let's not forget what Damien did to Tasha."

Coco drew in a breath. She'd known York's murdered girl-friend. "I'm going to have to agree with Roy on this one, sis," Coco said. "He's liable to get laser focused on finding Gustov and lose sight of the objective."

"Which is?" RJ asked.

"Finding their next target." She was again back to the main screen, clicking on folders. "I think I found something."

She'd opened a folder filled with maps and grids. It opened onto the screen, a layout of what looked like a military base.

"Where is this?" RJ asked.

"I don't know. It looks like an air force base."

Indeed, running across the lower section was a long runway.

Another shot gave an aerial view.

"I know that base," Roy said quietly.

RJ looked at him.

"I was sent there after I was rescued in Afghanistan. They have a hospital there, and it's under the radar. A lot of spec ops guys end up there instead of Germany. Because, well, spec ops."

A chill went through RJ. "Where is it?"

"Italy. Sigonella, Italy. It's an Italian base that works with the US Navy. It's also our forward operating base for flights into Syria and, really, anywhere in the Middle East that we'd like to take a good look at. Maybe drop a few reminders."

Oh. "So, important then."

"Not more important than any other base, but, yes, if you add to it how many spec ops guys stop over."

"Any carriers or battleships in the area?"

He lifted a shoulder. "Send this to Logan. He'll get an answer to that."

"An answer to what?"

The voice came from behind her, and she turned to see York emerging from the bedroom, buttoning his shirt over his bandage. It looked like he'd showered, his blond hair in spikes, his face freshly shaven. He was barefoot, though, and wearing a pair of jeans.

He came over to them, rolling up his sleeves. "What's that?" He leaned over the computer.

Coco had closed the images of Rulan Gustov. The omission sat in RJ's chest, but maybe Roy and Coco were right.

Damien Gustov had destroyed York's life, chased him, killed people he loved, and even tried to kill her. So yeah, knowing he had a brother out there, weirdly connected to their current situation...so much for his retiring to a hamlet in the middle of Washington.

Maybe that was just a silly dream, anyway.

She spun the ring around her finger, diamond down as York peered into the screen.

"We cracked the computer security," Coco said. "It's Sigonella Naval Air Station, in Italy."

"Huh." He stood up and ran his hand through his hair, clearly still waking up. "Tea anywhere?"

"Over on the counter. And croissants," Roy said.

"Gotta love Paris." He fought a yawn.

"I'm going to download the contents of the hard drive onto my computer," Coco said. "Then, you should package it up and send it to Logan."

"Will do," RJ said.

"By the way, did you guys hear about the plane crash?" Coco picked up a Diet Coke. "I was surfing twitter while the program was loading—did you know that Winchester Marshall's plane went down?"

RJ stilled. "What?"

"Yeah. Apparently, it was his publicity crew. Just fell out of the sky." She finished off the coke. "Wyatt says that you guys are related."

"Sorta. Is he...did he die?"

"No. He was on a different flight—earlier. Apparently, the plane had mechanical issues, so he hopped a commercial flight earlier in the day. He issued a statement from Rome last night. So sad, though. He's taking some time off his tour, I guess."

She sat back, glanced at Roy.

The plane.

It felt too close, too personal.

Why would Ruslan Gustov target Winchester Marshall's plane? The whole thing had a connection and, in her gut, she couldn't help but feel like maybe that connection was pouring himself a cup of coffee.

Or worse, hiding a diamond ring on her finger.

RJ looked at Roy. He shook his head.

Oh, she felt sick. But maybe they were right.

Focus.

Next stop, Italy.

CHAPTER
EIGHT

If York were to propose all over again, it would be today. At one of the cute seaside trattorias overlooking the Mediterranean Sea in the beach side town of Catania, Italy, on the island of Sicily.

Overhead, a few clouds shifted in the endless blue sky. Seagulls strutted along the beach, stealing treats from sunbathers who lounged in a cordoned off area that local hotels had commandeered. Children chased each other around the chairs, holding popsicles while a few parents tried to ignore them.

In the distance, the tall masts of sailboats cut through the horizon, moored between powerboats in a quaint marina.

"I can't believe they aren't doing anything." RJ shook her head, still wound up, maybe, from their conversation with Captain Parker, the commander of the Sigonella Naval Air Station.

The fact they'd even gotten an audience with the Captain sorta blew his socks off—he knew that Logan had probably gone right to President White for that permission. Still, York felt a little silly with the dire warning that he, Roy and RJ had suggested to the commander, the idea that some rogue force wanted to take out the tiny Naval Air Station. Sure, it was the Navy's only air station, and yes, the point of attack for the Middle East, but of course the military had thought through any attacks, including chemical, cyber and EMP. All affected on base devices were behind Faraday cages and thank you so much, they'd keep a lookout, but you can show yourselves out.

York, for one, was ready to go home.

Or maybe, as long as their vacation in Paris was cut short, to head up to Tuscany, as long as they were in Italy and maybe spend a few days at a villa.

Maybe find a magistrate, one who could cut through the red tape and marry them.

Now, as he and RJ walked along the boardwalk heading for a hotel bistro, the smell of the sea thick in the air, he dearly hoped she could let it go and focus on their future.

"I'm sure that whoever is behind this knew the military protected their equipment—it's the United States Military for Pete's sake. So then, there's something we're not thinking of. What about all those fighter jets and C-130s on the tarmac?"

"Babe. You gotta let it go." He'd tried to distract her with a stroll around the city today, losing themselves in the ancient architecture and quaint cobblestone streets. Geraniums spilled out of terracotta planters along stone sidewalks, or above, from balconies with wrought iron balustrades. And some pistachio gelato helped get them—him, at least—back into the vacation vibe.

They'd arrived in Catania last night after a grueling day of travel—from Charles De Gaulle to Rome to a hopper over to Sicily. Mt Etna had erupted a couple years ago, and the remains of the lava and subsequent earthquake still scarred the northern part of the island. To his memory, Hamilton Jones and a few of the guys from Jones, Inc. had been here for that little adventure.

York was over adventures, thank you. He'd done his part, warned the appropriate people, and frankly, he just wanted a nice, calm dinner with the woman he loved.

His stomach growled, despite the arancini that he'd purchased from a street vendor a couple hours ago. After the gelato.

"How can I let it go when it just doesn't feel right in my gut?"

Oh. Because her gut was too often right. She'd been the one who unraveled the conspiracy to kill the president. And it had been her gut that propelled her to travel across the pond and into Russia to save a General from assassination.

Problem was, her gut wrote checks that York usually ended up paying.

"I know. But what else can we do?" He pulled her out of the way of a skateboarder zipping down the boardwalk.

"I don't know. But definitely not give up. Not go home. What about Mads? He has a daughter who needs him. And how can you just let Martin run around loose?"

Her words burned in his chest.

No. Not his problem.

But his mouth tightened.

"We missed something, and I want to find it."

He was starting to lose his appetite. Roy had left them shortly after their meeting with Parker, vanishing as quickly as he appeared. Maybe—probably—searching for Martin. And answers. He'd show back up when he had something.

Maybe.

Or maybe York could simply leave this in Roy's hands.

"York?"

He glanced at her. What was he going to say, that the

nightmares of his past had caught up to him, and that the worst of them included not only cutting Claire's broken body down, but the memory of how close he'd come to losing RJ the exact same way.

He blew out a breath.

A horn tweeted, and RJ pushed him off the boardwalk, landing with him in the sand.

A kid on a scooter drove by. York scrambled to his feet, breathing hard. "Seriously? We're walking here!"

The kid didn't even look back and York fought the crazy urge to run him down, maybe remind him that pedestrians had the right of way.

RJ pressed a hand to his arm. "It was an accident."

He looked at her. "He could have killed us."

"Killed is a little strong. Sprained an ankle, maybe."

He walked away from her, onto the beach. Stared at the sea. Fishing boats rode the gentle waves, the Ionian Sea such a deep, tranquil blue he nearly wanted to keep walking.

"You okay?" RJ touched his back and he stiffened.

So, maybe not.

She put her arms around him. After their showdown at the base, they'd returned to their hotel—he's snagged adjoining rooms at Le Dune, a hotel right off the beach—she'd changed into a pretty black sun dress, a hat, a pair of sandals. Now, the wind whispered her dark hair around her face, those blue eyes worried as they searched his.

Fine. "The nightmares are back."

Her eyes widened. "Oh."

"I thought, after we caught Martin, and shut down the assassination plot they'd go away—and they did for a while. They do. When we're in Shelly. When I know you're safe."

"York."

"I know. But...I'm right back there, Claire's blood on my

hands, and then, all I can think about is you hanging from that rope—"

"But you saved me."

"What if I hadn't gotten there in time!" He didn't mean to shout, or maybe he did. But he slid his grip onto her arms. "Roy said something I can't shake—that you're not afraid to risk your life because I'll always be there to save you. But...what if I'm not. What if I can't get there?"

She took a step back. "York, you don't have to protect me."

He stared at her. "Yes. Actually. Yes, I do."

Her mouth opened. Closed. Then, "No. I can take care of myself."

Oh, he didn't want to argue with her. "I know you're smart and capable and...whatever. Forget I said anything."

"No. I mean—York, terrible things happen to people every day. We were just nearly run over by a scooter. It doesn't mean we run and hide—"

"I'm not hiding! I'm just..." He reached for her hand. "I don't know why, but deep down inside, I can't help but believe that if we walk away, start a new life in Shelly, the nightmares will end. I can put the past behind me. Us."

She swallowed.

"Listen, I just...can we just go home, RJ? Paris was a bad idea, I get that now."

She studied him for a moment, then finally nodded. "Yes."

Yes? His breath gusted out. Yes.

She stepped in and wrapped her arms around his neck. "I get it. Let's go home."

He closed his eyes, her words winding inside him.

Home.

She leaned back. "But not before you feed me."

He touched his hands to her face, his thumbs caressing her cheeks. "I love you."

"I love you, too," she said quietly.

He slipped his hand back into hers and headed back to the boardwalk. He had picked a restaurant a few blocks from their hotel that had a deck that overlooked the ocean. He'd asked the hostess, when he made the reservation to seat them near the beach.

She found them a table overlooking the marina. Powerboats, catamarans, and sailboats listed at their moorings, white and beautiful against the blue sky.

RJ slid in opposite him, her view to the marina, his to the beach and the boardwalk, the stretch of beach they'd just walked.

"I wish I could propose all over again. I kind of botched it last time."

She smiled. "Go ahead."

"RJ, you are the most amazing, beautiful, smart woman I've ever met. Brave and yes, sometimes too curious..."

She grinned at him. "Appropriately curious."

"You found me out."

"Hardly."

"Completely. And you stayed with me even when you saw the truth."

She leaned forward. "I also saw the man you wanted to be." The wind stole her hair.

"Yeah. And still want to be. I want to have a family with you, RJ. Build a life. Finally. So, again I ask...will you marry me?"

She laughed, and it was sweet and full and—

His phone rang.

He ignored it.

"What if it's Roy?" She let go of his hand and leaned back. "Get it." Her gaze went to the marina behind him.

He pulled out his phone. Oh, his realtor from Shelly. "I need to take this," he said.

She lifted a shoulder.

He got up and headed into the restaurant, answering on the way. "Nicole."

"Hey, York. Good news, the owner accepted your offer." She named the price. "And they want to close in 30 days."

"That'll do."

"I sent you a link for the earnest money."

"I'll get it done."

"You and RJ are going to love this place. It's so perfect for a family, and I know you wanted to be close to Jethro's house. So lucky that he knows the owner."

"Agreed. Thanks, Nicole."

"Congratulations."

He hung up and opened his bank app, moved money into the escrow account via the link she'd sent him.

The afternoon sun hung low on the sea, and he watched the rose gold sky for a moment, the way the rays touched the blue water, turning it shiny and bright.

Then he turned back to the deck.

Stilled.

RJ wasn't at the table.

He quick walked around the tables, to their spot.

Her chair was pushed out, her water glass half full, but no sign of her. He turned and searched the deck. Maybe she went to the bathroom.

Sinking down in his chair, he picked up his menu. Perused it and decided on a shrimp pasta.

The waitress came over. "A drink for you, sir?"

He paused, then, "Just a glass of Sauvignon Blanc—no, make that two, one for my fiancée."

"Very good," she said.

Fiancée. Soon, wife. So maybe this trip wasn't a wash.

The sun had settled lower, gold bleeding out over the water, turning red at the edges.

The waitress returned with his wine. He sipped it, watching kids run into the waves, back out. The table next to him got their food. Smelled so good he nearly leaped for it.

He checked his watch. Huh.

Maybe...

Call him paranoid, but certainly it didn't take a woman fifteen minutes to go to the bathroom.

The waitress came by and refilled his water.

"You didn't happen to see my fiancée leave, did you?"

"No, sir."

Right. He got up and felt not just a little foolish as he made his way to the ladies' room. A woman emerged, and he asked her if there was anyone matching RJ's description—dark hair, black sun dress— in the room.

"Just me," she said, and with those words everything inside him went cold.

He returned to the deck, hope thick in his chest.

No RJ.

What. The...

He stared out at the beach, scanning it, then turned and studied the marina.

Just a power boat headed out to sea.

"Are you all right, sir?" His waitress, holding a fresh basket of bread.

His throat thickened. "No. I don't think I am."

She was coming right back. Really. RJ just needed a closer look because the man looked so much like—well, it had to be Abu Massuf standing out on that dock talking with some yacht owner.

She noticed him right about the time York's phone rang, and then he'd gotten up and walked away and he was taking so long and then the man—dark skin, jeans, a white shirt—started walking away and what if this was their one, their only chance, to really find out what was going on?

So, she'd shot a look at the restaurant—no York—and then...but she really would be *right back*.

She probably should have picked up a burner phone in Paris, but there'd been no time, and those words had come out of her mouth when she talked to Roy. *I'm not going anywhere without York.*

Yeah, well she'd also said she'd learned her lesson, so apparently, she'd been lying to herself a little.

But really. *Right. Back.*

She just needed to find out who he was talking to, and where he was going, and maybe even where he was staying so that she could track down poor Mads.

RJ hustled along the boardwalk, the short distance to the pier, her eyes on Abu. He had exited the long dock, and she made a mental note to find out what slip number he'd been standing at—fourth from the end—and then slowed so she didn't cross paths with him.

Good thing she wore a hat and a dress, and looked completely different from the last time she'd trailed him, although she didn't think he'd seen her then, either.

The sun had started to set, a low simmer behind the buildings, the rays stretching out across the water, turning it dark bronze. The wind caught the smells of the harbor—seawater, brine, oil.

It had been such an amazing afternoon with York. Romantic. And his words on the beach about the nightmares just sat inside her and twisted.

She knew them well. Had been with him a few times when he'd woken in an airplane seat next to her, or even on the sofa in the next room of a hotel suit, shouting. Sweating. Shaking.

Remembering. Even, reliving the past.

And it wasn't just Claire's death he relived, but RJ's near death, the time Gustov and York's traitorous ex-CIA boss had kidnapped her, tied a rope around her neck, and threated to hang her. Had beaten York as he tried to save her life.

Yeah, that was a nightmare that sometimes found her, too.

So, okay. Yes. She got it. His need to put it behind him. To hide, as she put it.

And maybe that was the right answer. Really.

Because she loved him.

But she also knew him, and frankly, there was no way she believed he was okay with just letting Alan Martin walk away. Okay with turning his back on a potential bomb that could... well, the scenarios turned her cold.

And made her scramble across the road, just before the light turned red.

She ducked into the door of a bakery, and for a moment, her stomach churned at the smells of Bomboloni stacked on trays in the front window. This was taking too long—poor York might be back to the table by now.

When she peeked out again, Abu was further down the street.

She scrambled out and the whole thing felt familiar. *Don't lose him. Don't get caught.*

He crossed the street, and continued down another block, and they passed another resort on the water, a couple boutique hotels and only then did she hear the rumble of a plane overhead. Pausing in the street, she watched as, not too far away in the distance, a jet swooped down and landed beyond her eyesight.

What?

She kept walking and watched Abu cut through a parking lot, away from the sea. Ducking behind cars, she followed. He didn't even turn around, but then again, the mirrors could betray her, right?

She tracked him out of the parking lot and down a rutted sidewalk, past chain fencing and more parking lots. She scampered into the shadow of a thick smooth tree trunk. Across the street, and a hundred yards from wire fencing sat a wide tarmac. Hangers and a tower rose in the distance.

And parked in front of them, commercial planes.

Gooseflesh raised on her skin.

Switching her gaze back to Abu, she managed to spot him just as he disappeared into an orange two-story building set back from the road via a parking lot.

Picking up her pace, she stopped on the outskirts of the parking lot and stationed herself behind an old Fiat. The lot was crowded with cars. A painted guard house sat near the gated entrance.

Probably long-term parking for the airport.

She searched the lot.

Bingo. She spotted the gray van from Sézanne in the back corner and her heart slammed into her chest.

She'd found them. See, this is what curiosity got you.

She had to get back to the restaurant, tell York. Maybe get a hold of Roy.

Because it just ate her up that Captain Parker hadn't given their story even a moment's consideration. Didn't he realized that they might be saving lives? American lives?

But first...she slipped out from her hiding place, strolled

out the gate and casually meandered past the building. Glanced at the name. *Catania Fly Hotel.*

So, not super original, but it did afford them a view of the airport.

And, striking distance, if they aimed their weapon at the right plane. But why disable it as it was taking off, or landing?

She paused in the next parking lot, turned, and hid behind a dumpster.

What about Mads? Studying the building, she noted a balcony over the front entrance, and a fire escape style stairway that curved around the back.

She could just—

What if I can't get there?

York's voice threaded through her.

No. She didn't need York to save her.

Still, it was stupid to go blindly into a situation that involved international terrorists, right?

She turned and practically jogged through the next few parking lots until she came to a side street. She followed it back to the road, and then took that back to the ocean.

Came out on the main street, the ocean turning dark under the fading sunlight.

Turning, she headed back to the marina. Lights sparkled from the deck of the restaurant.

But before she hit the boardwalk back to their table, she walked out on the dock, down to the fourth slip from the end.

A forty-foot yacht was tied up to the mooring, the name Andiamo etched on the back. It sat in darkness, but even from here, she could make out the flybridge, the massive front deck.

Big enough to mount a Marx-device on it and shoot something out of the sky. Because she'd done the math on her walk back to the beach.

The best target would be a plane *about* to land, or just after takeoff, when they most needed their computer for flight.

Music twined from the deck of the restaurant as she climbed the stairs, a violinist who wound her way around the tables.

Yes, it was a romantic night, the perfect night for their last epic adventure. She didn't really expect them to stop whatever was happening, but she could tell Roy, and then maybe she—and York—could sleep in peace.

She stilled ten feet from their table.

A young couple sat where she and York had sat only...she looked at her watch.

An hour ago.

Oh. No.

She turned, and nearly ran into a waitress. "Oh!"

The woman clearly recognized her because after she steadied the glasses on her tray she glanced at the couple, then back to RJ. "He left."

Right. Of course.

"Thank you."

Oh. Wow. She should have left him a note, or maybe...

But if she had waited for him, Abu would have escaped. Now, she'd figured out their plan, or at least had found the gray truck and...

Oh boy.

The restaurant wasn't far from their hotel—just down the boardwalk—and she began to run as the sun slipped behind the buildings, leaving behind a mottled purple sky.

She didn't have a key card but managed to squeeze into the door of their quaint two-story building behind another couple. Quick walked across the tile to the stairs and rushed up them while the couple called the lift.

The quaint hotel was only three stories, and York had

gotten them adjoining rooms. Her feet slapped on the tile as she walked down the hall, her heart thundering. *I'm sorry, but wait until I tell you what I found!*

Or maybe she'd just start with *I'm sorry*, full stop, period.

She stopped at his door, cleared her throat, took a breath.

Knocked.

The door opened.

York stood there, his jacket off, his blue eyes ferocious, his chest just rising and falling.

"I'm sorry. I saw—"

"You left."

Funny that he wasn't reaching out to grab her hand, to pull her into himself like last time. He simply stood there.

"Can I come in?"

He held open the door.

She slipped inside and stood against the wall as he closed the door. Palmed his hand on it. He hung his head, took a breath.

Oh. He wasn't just mad, he was *furious.*

"York. I'm sorry."

He didn't look at her.

"I found Abu. He was at the marina talking to this guy who owns a yacht—the Andiamo. I saw he was leaving—and you weren't there, so I panicked. And followed him, and I know I probably should have waited for you, but I didn't want to lose him so..."

He drew in a long breath.

Then he stood up and walked away from her.

Standing at the window, he shoved his hands into his pockets. His shoulders rose and fell, his back tight.

"Did you hear me? I found Abu. And the gray van."

"I can't do this, RJ."

She walked toward him. "I know. We'll call Roy. I'll tell him what I know. They're staying at a hotel near the airport called *Catania Fly Hotel*." Her hand touched his arm. His biceps were tight, his entire body a knot. "I think they're going to try to take down a bigger plane this time."

He was staring out the window. Said nothing.

"York?"

"This is how it's going to be, isn't it?"

"How *what* is going to be?"

He turned. His eyes glistened. "I can't...I..." He closed his eyes.

"York, I didn't realize it would take so long."

He held up his hand, his eyes opening. "No. No, that's not okay." He took a breath. "I waited for you. I went to the ladies' room. I searched the restaurant. And then I thought...I thought maybe Martin or Abu had found you and then...then..." His jaw tightened and he turned away.

And then, her hands went to her mouth as he cleared the desk. The phone, the lamp, the brochures flew across the room. The phone hit the wall, the lamp crashed onto the floor and York walked away shaking.

Oh my.

"I scared you," she said softly.

He rounded on her. "Scared isn't even in the same galaxy."

Oh.

"The thing is, RJ, I think finally, I'm catching on. I'm starting to realize why you drove your brothers crazy, why they always had to keep an eye on you."

His accusation was a knife, and suddenly, the old words rose, the ones she'd thrown back at her over-protective arrogant brothers for twenty-some years. "I told you that you don't have to protect me!"

"I *always* have to protect you, RJ! Always. Because you don't protect yourself!" His eyes were on fire.

She sharpened her voice. "Well maybe if I had the training I've been asking for—asking *you* to give me—then I wouldn't need you to rescue me!"

He stared at her, a ferocity in his gaze that could burn through her. "I'm not training you to live a life that will get you killed."

"I'm not going to die—"

"Everyone I love dies, RJ. *Everyone*. And you know that better than anyone." His voice had raised, and now he looked away from her, his jaw tight, as if trying to clamp down on the roil inside.

Her voice tightened. "I'm not Claire."

"Believe me, I know."

"What's that supposed to mean?"

He turned to her, and his eyes were wet. "Claire at least listened to me. She knew she didn't belong in the world I ran in. She stayed at home, took care of our son—"

"And yet they still died."

His mouth opened. Closed and something of pain flashed in his eyes.

No. Oh, wow, she didn't actually say that. "York." With everything inside her she wanted to reach out, pull the words back. "I'm sorry—"

"Nope, you're right." He held up his hand. "In fact, that's my point exactly. We keep living this life, and it will turn on us. It will find us. And it will take you from me in the most horrific of ways." He swallowed. "And I can't stick around and watch that."

She blinked at him. "Wait. What...what do you mean?"

He stepped away from her, held his hands up. "It's over, RJ. I...I'm out. I can't fight this and win. I realize now that you don't want Mack, the small-town guy. You want Jack Powers—"

"York."

"The problem is, I don't want to be the man you saw in Russia, or even last year in America. I'm...I can't be that guy anymore."

What? She stared at him, her chest emptying, her knees soft. "Wait...what?"

"I'm going back to America. If you...if you want me, then you know where I'll be."

"York."

"If I'm not around, then well...I won't have to watch you die."

Then he turned and headed toward the door.

"Where are you going?"

"I don't know. But my phone is on the dresser. Call Roy and tell him what you saw." He stood at the door, his hand on the knob. Turned to her. Met her eyes.

His voice dropped, soft, matter of fact. "I loved you. And yes, I would have died for you—still would, RJ. Every day, every minute. But you...you run after trouble like it might be a drug. And it...it slays me." He opened the door. "Your key card is in your room. Lock your door behind you."

Then he left.

Just. *Left.*

She stood there, her heart a fist in her chest.

No, this couldn't be right. No—

She took a breath. Glanced at the door. Then at the phone. Walked over to it and scooped it up.

She'd call Roy, and then—

What was she *thinking?*

"York!"

She turned and fled out the door after him. He'd already disappeared down the stairs.

She took off, hit the stairs, took them down and ran through the lobby.

Out onto the street.

Night had fallen, just the light over the door of the hotel casting out into the sidewalk. She looked both ways, spotted the dark frame of a man stalking away. "York!"

She took off, running.

And then, she was flying, her foot caught on something sticking out from the ground. She landed, and cried out, scrubbing her hands, her knees, landing on all fours.

Oh. What an idiot. Tears burned her eyes. He was right. She did run after trouble.

I'm sorry, York.

And then an arm snaked around her waist, pulling her up. She wanted to weep as she found her feet, as she turned into her rescuer, realizing, painfully, the truth of York's words.

I *always have to protect you—* "I'm sorry—I'm so..."

"Shh."

She jerked her head up, her eyes wide. Drew in a breath.

"I'll take care of you now."

Her scream was cut off by Alan Martin slamming his hand over her mouth.

She struggled against him, but it didn't matter because in a moment, the gray van pulled up, a hood blanketed her head and then all she knew was the hard interior of the van floor against her back, duct tape around her hands and feet and the sense that the only thing she desperately wanted was for York to come and rescue her.

CHAPTER
NINE

He should turn around.

York knew it even as he took the stairs two at a time, practically running from the woman who... okay, fine, of course he loved her. But never had a woman tied him up in a knot like RJ did.

She *wasn't* like Claire. Not even a little.

More like Tasha. And look how that had turned out. His own words pinged back at him.

Everyone I love dies, RJ. Everyone.

His chest burned, a little ragged with that omission as he hit the dark street, stalking out into the darkness.

He just needed a...moment. Just a breath.

Because, was he really going to go back to Shelly alone?

Probably not.

Maybe.

Oh, his own stupid ultimatum turned to fire in his throat.

Because really, how was he supposed to live with himself if something happened—

A cry lifted behind him, and every bone in his body turned to liquid.

He'd know that scream anywhere.

RJ!

He'd already stalked down to the next block, but as he turned, in the dim, wan light of the hotel, he made out shapes.

Two people struggling.

He took off running, a shout in his own throat as the bigger shape pushed the smaller into a vehicle.

"Hey!"

It took off from the curb, coming toward him.

He ran straight at the van, caught the passenger side mirror, jumped onto the running board, then reached for the handle of the sliding door.

Unhooked it.

The side door slid open, even as the van swerved, trying to dislodge him. But he reached inside, found the seatbelt strap of the front passenger, and used it to swing himself inside.

He landed on the bed, but in a second, a fist slammed against his face. He jerked, his grip still on the seatbelt. The blow cleaned his clock, but he rebounded blindly, kicking out.

Met flesh. Whoever hit him fell back.

The van sped under a streetlight, and he got a good glimpse of the cargo.

A woman in a dress lay on the cargo floor, her hands and feet duct taped, her head covered.

"RJ!"

She jerked at his shout, sat up, fighting her bonds.

Good girl. He leaped for her.

But his attacker had found his feet and sent a knee into his gut.

The air huffed out of York, and he dropped to his knees, gasping.

And then the man kicked him. A shot across the face that had him tumbling back.

He fell half out of the open door and scrabbled for a hand-hold. Grabbed the edge of the door just before he fell headfirst into the pavement.

A hand grabbed his shirt, pulled him up.

They passed under a streetlight, and the light flashed on his face.

Alan Martin. What—?

His old friend looked at him, dark eyes in his. "Now we're having fun."

York headbutted him, but Martin jerked back. A miss.

He rounded with a fist—it caught York's chin and the world spun.

York landed hard on the deck, rolled and kicked Martin in the face. The man reeled back.

But the passenger had launched into the back and landed on York, his knee in his chest.

In the dim light, as he fought off the man's blows, he thought he saw—wait—Damien?

The thought hiccupped through him, and in that moment, the man landed a hit. Blood filled his mouth.

Next to him, RJ was still fighting, her legs now free. He reached for her, but the Damien lookalike grabbed his hand, wrenched it back, and then Martin was back in the game, and they were flipping him over.

No.

He rolled, caught the lookalike in the face with a kick, then grabbed RJ's bound hands. "C'mon RJ!"

He bounced to his feet, trying to jerk her up when the van took a left turn, hard. The momentum jerked his grip free, and he bounced against the front passenger seat.

Then, as he watched, Martin grabbed RJ, his arm around her throat.

York righted himself, breathing hard.

He wasn't leaving this carnival ride without her.

The blow hit him at his side, a kick that jerked him off his feet and then...

Then he was flying. Out of the door, into the air until he fell like a brick onto the road.

He rolled, then scrabbled to his feet, not feeling any pain. "RJ!"

Then he took off running after the van, his heart thundering inside him.

It sped off, outdistancing him, and after another block, he slowed, breathing so hard he might be stroking out.

He leaned over, grabbed his knees, then gave up and collapsed, shaking.

But he couldn't stop the shout, the growl, the ache of frustration that roiled through him into the night.

He leaned his face down, almost onto the pavement, trembling with the force of it.

If he hadn't walked away—

Breathe.

Just. *Breathe.*

And now the pain came because of course he'd torn his stitches, banged up his knee good, and blood filled his mouth. He spat it out on the ground.

He should have gotten a license plate number.

Except, Roy had it, didn't he, from his adventure in Sézanne?

York pushed himself up, still shaking.

Then he turned and started running back in the direction they came. He followed the moonlight, the sounds of the sea and finally found the street he'd been doing his leaving on.

The hotel's entrance light sprayed out on the sidewalk, the only reason he didn't miss the cell phone—his cell phone—laying on the sidewalk.

He picked it up, still breathing hard.

She'd fallen here. Because she'd been running after him.

Because he'd given up. Walked away.

Because he'd been a coward.

He ground his jaw, gripped the cell phone, and headed inside.

Think, York.

He took the stairs two at a time and found the door to their room open, evidence of RJ's flight after him.

Bile filled his chest.

He shut the door, walked to the window, stared out at the dark sea, the moon now dragging a finger of hot white through it, and dialed Roy.

"York?"

"Martin took her."

A soft word of frustration.

"I don't know why, but now he has her and..." York clenched his fist, trying not to put it through the wall. "Tell me you got a plate number?"

"For what?"

"The van!"

A beat. "Are you sure it was the same van?"

"No, I'm not sure, but call it a hunch since Martin was there. And a guy who looked—no, it's crazy. Just adrenaline."

"Looked like who?"

"No one. Do you have that license plate number?"

"Yes. We already ran the plates. It was stolen."

And now he wanted to throw the phone.

"What happened?"

He skipped the fight, the ultimatum. "I was...I left for...I needed air. And RJ came after me, and then I heard her scream. By the time I got there, the van had pulled away. I managed to get in it, had a little scuffle." He had walked to the mirror. Blood caked on his split lip, and a lift of his shirt showed a deepening bruise on his ribs. He lifted it more and miraculously the stitches had held, but the wound oozed blood.

He dropped the shirt. "Why RJ?" Although he knew the answer.

Because of him. *Everyone I love dies, RJ.* Everyone.

Sinking on the bed, he cradled his head in his hand. "He'll kill her."

"We'll find her." Roy's voice had dropped.

York shook his head, looked at his mug in the mirror.

He should have known better than to think he could put the past to rest.

"Why did you need air?"

Oh. He shook his head. "I was angry. She'd taken off again and...I said things."

"Taken off?"

"She said she saw Abu at the marina."

"What marina?"

"We were at a beachside restaurant not far from our hotel. I stepped out to take a phone call and when I came back, she was gone. I....it...anyway, she showed back up at the hotel about an hour later."

"Sorry, man."

Him too. He made a sound, deep in his chest.

"Did she find him?"

"Abu? Yes. Or so she thinks. She followed him to a hotel near the airport."

"The Catania airport?"

"Apparently."

"But what about the marina?"

150

"She said something about a boat. The Andiamo."

"Just a sec."

He didn't know where Roy was, but clearly near resources because in a moment —

"The Andiamo is a 40-foot yacht owned by a Turk named Ahmet Balik. He's in shipping and has a home in Greece."

"What's his connection to Abu?"

"None that I can see. But according to maritime records, the Andiamo is in port in Catania. Did she tell you anything else?"

Nothing he wanted to share with Roy.

"Okay, I'll meet you at the marina. Let's track down the Balik fellow and see if he can lead us to Abu. In the meantime, I'll ask Coco to check the various hotels for Abu. Maybe he checked in under an alias."

Roy was in town. York didn't know why that made the knot in his gut loosen, but...

I'll find you, RJ. I promise.

Roy, apparently, read his mind. "We'll find her, York."

He gave a sound of assent and hung up.

Then he took a minute to clean up—ran a cloth over his face, pulled on a clean black tee-shirt, jeans.

In another minute he was out the door. He'd pulled on a black hoodie and yanked up the hood. Just in case he didn't need to be noticed.

The moonlight cast over the white-hulled boats sitting on mooring balls or tied to the long docks at the marina. The water had stilled, silver tipping the water. He had run over, so he didn't expect Roy to meet him, but the man was standing in the shadows near the locked entrance. He too wore a black tee-shirt, jeans and a jacket.

"Where have you been?"

"Why? Miss me?" Roy grinned, and it was such an odd look, York had nothing.

Something had put Roy in a good mood. It instantly vanished, however, when he turned to the locked gate. "Did you bring my lock pick set?"

York pulled it out of his pocket. "Never leave home without it."

Roy pulled out the instruments and went to work on the lock. In seconds the gate creaked open.

All the while, RJ's words burned inside him. *I want you to teach me how to do that.*

Roy slipped inside. York followed him. They crept down to the dock and Roy pulled out a penlight. He shined it on the hulls of the boats as they walked down the pier. Nothing that matched the Andiamo's name or description.

"Let's try the next one," he said and, of course, that made sense—it was the pier closest to the restaurant. York needed to get his head in the game.

Roy shined the light on the hulls again, but York was looking at the restaurant, and where they'd been sitting.

"Go to the end. The tables would have obscured the view of these boats. It has to be one of the far boats." He took off, jogging to the end of the dock. As he went, the vessels got bigger—from mono-hull sailboats to motor yachts to catamarans, and one very large super yacht moored at the very end.

Roy came up beside him. "No Andiamo."

But York had stopped at an empty slip. "What was here?"

Roy shot his light over an oil slick that puddled the dark water. "There was something here, not too long ago."

Movement, something thick in the water bumped against the pilings. Roy shot his light over to it and York's heart nearly stopped.

A plastic bag. But not just a bag, something wrapped in the

bag, duct taped and left behind. It bobbed in the water near the end of the narrow walkway between slips.

He strode over to it.

"York."

But he couldn't stop himself, the what-if's simply shutting down his brain.

He reached for the bag, got his hand into it and tried to heave it up out of the water. Too heavy, but Roy was right there to grab the other end.

Together they rolled the package onto the dock.

York stepped back, swallowed. It was easily the size and shape of a body.

Roy pulled out a knife.

"Careful," York said.

"Bro. There's no chance that...that person is long dead."

York just stared, forcing himself to breathe as Roy cut open the plastic.

The body was face down, and long brown hair spilled out of the cut.

York turned, gripped his knees, and retched into the water.

Oh God. Please—

"It's not her, York. It's a man."

Roy had turned him over. Sure enough, a man, maybe mid-forties, long hair knotted around his gray face. "He's been dead for a while." He shined his light along the body, now exposed in the bag. The man was still clothed, and Roy shot the light on his hand. "Married."

The relief could turn York lightheaded. He kneeled, his gut still queasy, but took a closer look at the ring. "It's silver, and this brownish stone looks like zultanite." He looked up at Roy. "Native to Turkey."

Roy sighed. "I guess we found our yacht owner."

York stood up and stared out into the sea. The dark sky fell into the horizon, blurred by the night. "I'm going to need a boat."

Oh, he was right. York was *so* right and RJ, if she lived through this—well, she probably wasn't going to live through this, so why make stupid vows.

Still, York was in her head. *We keep living this life, and it will turn on us. It will find us. And it will take you from me in the most horrific of ways.*

That and his shout—her name—as he fought with the men in the van. How he'd managed to find her, get inside the vehicle seemed nothing short of superhero, but there he was, fighting to save her.

Because he just couldn't help but show up.

And no, she couldn't see through the hood, just heard the grunts, the hits and kicks and then the terrible moment when he'd simply...vanished.

York?

Martin had cursed, in English, and Russian, then someone got hit.

The door slammed.

And she curled into a ball and prayed.

Please God, make me smart and brave. And help York find me.

Felt like a stupid prayer, especially since she'd gotten them into this mess, but hopefully God wouldn't hold that against her.

They hadn't driven long before they stopped and opened the doors and immediately, she knew.

The yacht. The smells of the sea drifted through her hood, and the freshness of the sea air settled onto her bare legs and when someone grabbed her arm, pulled her from the van and led her down to the dock, her feet clumped on the boards with a sound that she remembered.

They'd pulled the hood off just before they pushed her onto the boat, in the back end, and made her sit on a bench.

Across from her, also sitting on the bench, only untied, was Mads. He kept his head down, not looking at her.

"Mads?" she whispered.

He shook his head.

Okay.

Martin got in the boat next. "You just sit tight."

"He'll come for me."

"Oh, I'm counting on it."

She turned her face away. Shoot.

Another man climbed in, the one with the long hair—Ruslan, Damien's brother. He held a rag to his nose, and she wondered if that was York's handiwork.

The third man was Abu, and he went into the cockpit, then down into the cabins. A few moments later, he dragged out a large object in a plastic bag and it only took a couple thumps for her to realize—it was a body.

Abu tossed him overboard as Martin revved the engine and pulled away from the dock. They left the body in the water, floating in the slip.

And RJ really started to shake.

Brave. Smart. Please.

Overhead the stars spilled out across the sky, the moon nearly full as it hung over the water. The yacht sped up, bouncing over the slight waves.

While they traveled, Abu went back to the cabin and this time pulled up a suitcase.

Oh, Mads' suitcase, the one that looked like a 1930's bachelor's case.

He carried it along the edge of the boat to the front deck.

Ruslan came out and nudged Mads. Spoke in Russian, but RJ understood him. "It's time."

Mads got up, still not looking at her, and made his way to the front.

They'd left her alone. She looked over the side, at the distance to the water. Easy jump.

She just needed her legs and hands free.

And despite not wanting to teach her anything, hello, York had taught her how to get out of zip ties. Certainly, getting free of tape worked the same way. Glancing at Martin, still tucked away at the helm, she brought her hands up, then pulled her elbows down, hard.

It didn't snap. What?

She tried again. Nothing.

No, no, this wasn't...she brought the tape to her mouth, began to gnaw at it.

The boat was slowing.

C'mon, *work*—she tried the move again, this time harder.

The tape snapped.

Martin had brought the boat to a halt, the momentum driving her forward. She fell off the bench and caught herself with her hands.

Martin turned, his eyes on her. "Where do you think you're going?"

She turned over—why didn't she do her legs first?—and started to scramble for the side of the boat. Her hands gripped the edge, her legs on the bench—

"Oh no you don't!" Martin grabbed her around the waist and threw her on the deck. Stood over her. "I have plans for you."

She kicked at him, even as she scrambled back. "He'll kill you."

"He'll try. But he's getting rusty. All that time pouring drinks and flipping burgers. He's forgotten everything he knows."

She shook her head.

"Besides, he'll be so busy looking for you, he won't have time to find me."

Her eyes widened. "What do you mean?"

"You're smart. Figure it out." He grabbed her wrist and hauled her up. Sat her back on the bench and this time took a nearby rope and tied her wrists with it. "Sit still."

He shoved her back on the bench, then headed up to the front.

Tears burned her eyes because she got it.

Martin wasn't going to kill her—or maybe he would, and just hide her body, and poor York would spend every moment trying to find her.

Leaving Martin free to do whatever he wanted.

She was a liability, at best. An anchor at worst.

And just about the worst spy on the planet. She bit into the rope, trying to tug the knot free. Mads came back down the walkway and she lifted her head. He sat on the bench opposite her.

"What's happening."

He looked up at her. "I'm sorry."

Oh. "For what?"

"I didn't realize. I didn't...the device wasn't supposed to work."

"But it does work, Mads. And now what's happening?"

He shoved his hands between his knees and looked up in the sky. "It's a plane. They're waiting for a plane."

Her entire body chilled with his words. "What kind of plane? Passenger? Cargo?"

"I don't know. I just know it's landing in Catania or nearby and..." He lifted his head. "Listen, if I don't help them, they'll kill Hana." He looked at her then. "Maybe you can't understand this, but I can't be the cause of my daughter's murder."

"I do understand," she said.

He nodded.

"But we can't let them take down an airplane of people, Mads. That's just...that's wrong."

His jaw tightened.

"Tell me how to stop it."

He looked at her. Shook his head.

"Mads!"

"There's nothing!"

"What if we drown it. It can't work underwater, right?"

His eyes widened. Then, his voice cut low. "There is no time, even if we wanted to." He looked up.

In the distance, lights blinked, a plane somewhere over Greece, or maybe even Libya. Too far to guess, really.

Still. The stuff of nightmares.

"What's on the plane?"

"I don't know!"

She held up her hands. "Calm down."

First thing was to get her feet free. She leaned down, put her hands between her knees, then stood up and with everything she had, shoved her hands down, together, between her knees.

The force snapped the tape.

Yep, that's how it was supposed to happen.

Now, the rope. "Untie me!" She held out her hands.

He sucked in a breath.

"Don't be a pansy."

He knelt in front of her, fighting with the knot.

"Hey!"

She turned and spotted Ruslan headed down the walkway.

Uncanny how, in the dim light he looked like Damien, his dead brother. If she didn't know better—

Ruslan strode right up to Mads and hit him, *pow!*, across the face.

Mads fell back, his hand to his nose which erupted in blood.

"Stay down." Ruslan turned to her. Spat. "You move, you die. I don't care what Martin says."

Oh. But Martin had already let her into his plans, so no big surprise there.

Ruslan retrieved something from the cockpit, then slung it around his neck and climbed to the fly bridge.

Binoculars.

Her gaze went to the lights in the sky. They'd grown closer.

"How close does the target need to be?"

"Overhead, directly. Otherwise, it will be out of range."

Her gaze went to the cockpit. "So, if we can drive the boat out of range, it won't work?"

Mads looked at her, his mouth tight.

"I'll take that as a yes." Her teeth found the knot and she began to work it again. Mads had loosened it a little, maybe.

But in a moment, her jaw burned, and she'd made no headway. And people were going to die.

Around her, the sea was quiet, a few boats out, mostly sailboats, a few motor yachts. Maybe she should just scream for help.

And what—get more people killed?

She was staring out the back, still working on the stupid knot when she saw him.

Frankly, she nearly screamed.

Because, like some deep ocean creature, Roy simply raised his head out of the water. He wore no SCUBA apparatus, no snorkel, just a mask, and a wet suit.

159

And a knife.

He pulled himself aboard and in a second had unsheathed a dive knife and cut through her ropes. Put a finger to his mouth.

Then, he put his hands together and made a diving motion.

Right. Into the water with her. And Mads.

But Mads wasn't moving. Fine—she'd figure it out.

She grabbed Roy's arm. "The device is up front. They're taking out a plane."

He nodded, and then scooted up the walkway.

And she couldn't help a terrible gust of relief.

Until she saw Mads. He'd stood up, his gaze on Roy, as if—as if—

He took a breath, as if gearing up for a shout and she just...reacted.

Impulsive, just like York accused her of, but she launched herself at Mads.

He was a big man—not as big as York or Roy, but sturdy enough. Still, she was no lightweight and she had a running start.

She grabbed Mads around the waist and leaped off the boat.

He fought it—holding onto a bar, but she refused to let go, her arms, then legs around him and in a moment, his grip slipped. He careened into the water.

They went down, Mads on top of her, and she pushed him away from her, kicking hard.

She surfaced, gulping breaths. Looked around.

No Mads. But what was more, on the fore deck, Roy was waging war with Martin and Ruslan. And not losing.

But not winning, either, especially when Martin pulled out a knife.

Roy was fast, flicked it away, but didn't see the paddle that

Ruslan had procured, probably on his way down from the fly bridge.

He hit Roy broadside and maybe it was his wet feet, maybe a wave from a passing trawler, but RJ held in a shout as Roy tumbled off the edge into the sea.

No!

Next to her, she heard splashing—Mads, making for the boat.

"No, you don't!" She dove after him, grabbing him.

"Let me go!"

"They'll kill you!"

"I don't care!" He shoved her away.

And maybe he didn't mean to, but as he turned to the boat, he kicked her. His foot hit her face, broadside and just like that, the world shifted. She went down, gulped water, kicked up, found a breath, but it mixed with the water, and she coughed. More water in, and now she was retching, gagging, sinking—

"I got you."

Roy, behind her, his arm around her waist. "Just breathe."

She watched as Mads reached the boat. But he couldn't get a grip, the side too high to grab.

And then, the boat took off, cutting in an arc, heading back toward the mainland.

"What are they doing?" Roy treaded water to keep them afloat.

"Maybe they lost their window!" She looked up, and spotted the plane large, not quite overhead yet, but big enough to see it below the clouds.

Mads was hitting the water, shouting.

And then, a speedboat, something long and sleek zipped in beside them. "Roy! What happened?"

She looked up. York was at the helm, standing, one leg on his seat. "York!"

He looked at her. "You okay?"

She nodded. "Are you?"

"Now I am." He smiled at her.

And just like that, everything was okay, the darkness in her heart breaking free. Her eyes filled. *Oh, York, I'm so sorry—* that's what she wanted to say. Instead— "There's a bomb on that boat and it's going to take out that plane if you don't stop it!"

York looked up, found the plane, then spotted the boat.

Then he looked at her. "I'll be right back."

He gunned the boat, turning in the water and in a second, it motored off, kicking up a flume of water.

"It's a cigarette boat," Roy said. "A friend of Ham's let us use it." He let her go.

She treaded water, watching. In the darkness, not far away, Mads was also treading water, his face twisted.

What was York's plan? He probably should have picked up Roy if he wanted to board the boat, right?

Or maybe he was going to jump on—

And then she froze. "He's not going to—no, no—"

The boat wasn't slowing as it headed for the yacht. In fact, York had spun it out, around and with its speed, had turned the racing boat back towards the yacht.

"He's going to hit it. Head on!"

Roy grabbed her arm. "He's smart. Just—"

And then, it happened.

York simply rammed his boat, full speed into the yacht.

The explosion lit up the entire sky, a ball of fire and heat that plumed over the water.

And through the golden spray of light passed the airplane, wheels down, on final approach towards Catania.

CHAPTER
TEN

The only thing that mattered was that RJ was safe.

York had nearly blown the entire op by flashing on his lights and throttling the boat forward when she threw herself in the water, along with Mads—he assumed it was Mads. But she was a tough girl. A girl who knew how to swim. Still, he held his breath until he saw her head pop the surface.

And then, there was the tussle between her and Mads.

He didn't know what happened, but oh, he almost dove in after her. If not for Roy, who grabbed her, raised his hand above his head. *Everybody's okay.*

Except, by the way the yacht had fled the scene, mission not accomplished. Although, to his mind, they'd accomplished their mission op: rescue RJ.

Roy had added the part about grabbing Martin and his accomplices, getting their hands on the weapon.

Which meant, with RJ and Roy in the water, safely out of Martin's grip— "I'll be right back."

He liked this boat. Gorgeous. 42 feet long, 11-foot beam,

two thousand and fifty horsepower, it boasted five motors attached to the stern, a center helm with a raised seat—completely digital navigation and GPS system, with an automated sequential engine system.

He was nearly in love.

But, like he said, everything he loved died.

His chest still hurt, but it had started to open up a little. And, as soon as he'd motored away from RJ and Roy, he put the throttle down and spun the boat around.

Then he planed out and ate up the water to the yacht.

He'd already done the math, figured out the sacrifices, committed to them.

Already realized there would be a cost to take out Martin and whatever dire scheme he was into now.

And maybe that cost was him.

He passed the boat, flying past it, really, then slowed, turned, and set himself on a course to destruction.

Martin was on the front deck, holding on to the railing, looking up. Funny, maybe he didn't even see York.

But York saw him.

He put the throttle all the way down.

On the boat, the Marx device has started to glow, blue against the night. Faster—

RJ's words bounced around his head—*There's a bomb on that boat and it's going to take out that plane if you don't stop it!*

And who knew what was next? If Mads had developed a machine that could take out targets from the air...

Fifty feet, forty, thirty.

He flicked his lights on.

Martin jerked, turned, put his hand up to shield his eyes.

Twenty.

York leaped up on the seat.

Ten.

He dove off, plunging deep into the sea, kicking hard away from the plume of light that ballooned over him.

When he surfaced, the yacht was in flames, the deck blown to smithereens, the flybridge collapsing into the water.

And that's how it was done.

Around him, debris hit the water, and he ducked as burning decking showered down around him. He thought he could hear his name in the distance, but the fire was too loud, roaring.

Yes, he liked this. Probably too much. The win, the fact that maybe, just a little, he'd saved lives.

In the distance, a few boats had started over—a trawler, another yacht. He hoped that someone spotted Roy and RJ and Mads in the water.

The knife slipped in just below his ribs, in his back, probably ripping into his spleen. The next stab hit lower, right above his hipbone, and lodged there. Why Martin didn't just cut his throat, he didn't know, but as he pushed away, Martin turned the knife, ripping the wound open and York's entire body convulsed, pain lighting through him.

He grunted.

"That should slow you down," Martin said, then pushed him under.

York wanted to turn, to find the man, put his hands on him, but his body wouldn't respond, the pain shooting down his legs, through his torso. He kicked, made it to the surface, but couldn't hold it.

The water closed over his head.

He tried to reach behind him, to dislodge the knife, but it evaded his grip. He kicked again, managed a sip of air. Spotted a piece of wood and splashed for it.

C'mon, York. What's your major malfunction? His marine drill sergeant, in his head.

Sorry, sir. Yes, sir.

His hand closed around the piece of wood.

Too small—he brought it down with him when he sank.

He was losing blood—probably too much blood because the world started to spin. *Kick, York.* The water had turned frigid, his limbs numbing.

Kick!

He fought to the top, found air again and this time lights assaulted the yacht from the neighboring boats. *Lift a hand. Shout.*

But he had nothing.

He went under.

Maybe this was how it was supposed to end. He didn't imagine for himself a casual death—never had. And his regret had been reckoned with that day, as Mack, that he'd fallen on his knees at a small-town church altar. He wasn't without hope for Heaven.

But he would miss RJ.

Fight the battles you're assigned to fight.

He had. One by one. And maybe that fight was over.

Maybe the peaceful future he longed for was on the other side of eternity.

Still, the word thundered through him in the darkness.

Fight.

One last time. He kicked again, nearly spouting out a roar as it propelled him to the surface.

Hands caught him, pulled him up and his lungs nearly exploded.

"Gotcha," said a voice and he opened his eyes to see RJ, in the water, wearing a life jacket, holding him up, Roy on the other side, a flotation device under his arm. He hooked it around York.

"Nice fire."

He smiled, maybe.

"He's bleeding," RJ said. "He's got a knife in his back."

"Let's get him in the boat."

He closed his eyes as Roy pulled him through the water.

"Get the knife out of me," his voice came out a rasp.

"Not until we're aboard," RJ said. "You could bleed out."

Probably too late for that.

He spotted the lights of the trawler right before they dragged him to the fishing platform. Then hands pulled him aboard and he was set on the deck, face down.

More hands ripped away his shirt. "Please, take the knife out."

"Shh," RJ said. She put her face next to his on the deck.

Actually, the pain had started to subside, the chill setting in.

"We need a chopper!" Roy's voice. "Call Sigonella."

"Martin got away," he said.

RJ was looking at him, those blue eyes on his. "We'll find him."

He opened his mouth.

"Or not. Just breathe, York." She put her hand on his head.

"I'm afraid to close my eyes."

"Why?"

"Because...please, just...be here when I wake up."

"I'm not going anywhere." She pressed her lips to his. He wanted to reach up and touch her face, hold her there.

Instead, he closed his eyes.

And with everything inside him, tried to believe her.

"Coffee, RJ?"

She stood at the window in the waiting area down the hall from York's hotel room in the Sigonella Naval Hospital. The sun cascaded over the greening hills in the shadow of Mt. Etna, the volcano that rose, bold and glorious to the north.

She turned to Roy's voice and took the proffered cup. Blew on the steam rising from the surface before she took a sip. "Oh, that's bad."

"Sorry. It's all they had in the nurses' lounge." Roy sank into a brown vinyl chair that flanked the sofa she'd spent much of the night curled up on. Roy had slept. She hadn't, not with the nightmare of York's blood pooling on the deck of the boat, the way he'd passed out while they'd waited for the emergency flight.

He'd nearly died, his blood pressure so low that they'd had to shock his heart and flush him with six blood transfusions.

He'd gone into emergency surgery within moments of landing at Sigonella.

"Any update?"

"His blood pressure has stabilized, and he's breathing better. He lost his spleen, though. Thankfully the second stab didn't hit any major organs, but it tore up his back pretty badly. He's still unconscious."

She watched as the base came alive, sailors in BDUs and officer whites walking across the campus. To the south, at a separate base, fighter jets and other naval air machines were already deep into exercises. Even a few miles away, the entire building rumbled when a jet took off.

"Did you get a hold of Logan?"

"Yes. He managed to figure out the flight that we think they were targeting. Ironically, it wasn't landing at Catania."

She turned. "Really?"

"No. It was a 40-A clipper. Looks a lot like a commercial plane. Came in last night, classified flight."

"Did you get the manifest?"

"Yes. Logan is looking it over, but the initial report is that the passengers were doctors and infectious disease specialists from Africa—Nigeria, Kenya, Ghana, Uganda."

She took a sip of her coffee. "Why?"

"I don't know. But," he lowered his voice. "I heard that yesterday the director of the CDC was here, checking on their quarantine protocols."

"An outbreak of Ebola, maybe?"

"I don't know, and Logan didn't let on."

She sat down on the sofa. "Why would Martin want to take out a plane of African doctors?"

He shook his head. "We need to find him."

She looked at him, traced her thumb down the cup. "I think *you* need to find him. York and I...well, York needs a time out."

"I agree. That's why I booked you guys a couple weeks in Tuscany. It's a friend's place, but you'll love it."

Her mouth opened. "I thought...but you were the one who said I had to choose."

"Not today you don't." He took a sip of his coffee. Made a face. "Oh, it's like drinking mud water from some ditch in Benghazi. I should give it to Mads as a form of torture."

She cocked her head. "Go easy on him. His daughter is in the hospital."

"I know. I spent a good part of last night debriefing him. He's down the hall in another bed. I think he was in shock."

"I don't blame him. He's scared to death about his daughter."

"We need to go to Germany and get her."

She hadn't seen him come down the hall, but now Mads stood, dressed in a pair of white scrubs, barefoot, his blond hair askew. He looked like he'd been crumpled into a ball then hung out to dry, crackled and wrinkled.

"They'll be looking for you." Roy said to Mads' statement, his voice quiet.

"I don't care. I need to get my daughter." He looked at RJ. "And you have to come with me."

She sat up. "Me?"

"You got me into this." His mouth made a grim line. "If you hadn't followed me, broke into my hotel room, if you hadn't thrown me from the boat—"

"You'd be dead!"

He drew in a breath. "You said you could keep us safe. But now my daughter's life is in danger, and..." He ground his jaw. "And I'm not going to sit around and wait for them to murder her and throw her body from a bridge."

Oh. Well.

"I can't leave York." She shook her head. "I'm *not* going to leave him. Who knows what Martin is planning?"

"You must go!" Mads said. "You promised."

"I know, but—take Roy."

"No." Mads shot him a look, his mouth tightening. "He will scare her."

Agreed. Roy sorta scared everyone.

Roy had leaned forward, was considering his coffee. "I can't go."

Her heart stalled. "What?"

Roy's glance fell off Mads, settled on her. "Logan ordered me to stay with York."

She drew in a breath. But yes, she got that. Logan would want to protect York, one of his greatest assets. Still—"What about Hana?"

"I get it. If someone I loved was in trouble..." He paused, looked away, something pregnant and forlorn in his words. But silence settled on the end of them. "And maybe she'd respond better to a woman."

"York...he'd kill me if anything happened."

Roy leaned back. "I have a contact in Germany. She'll meet you at the hospital, make sure you get out safely. I'll call Logan and we'll get a flight to Heidelberg. You'll be in and out in an hour, back by tonight. He won't even know you're gone."

She blinked at him. "You're serious."

He finished off his coffee, then set the paper cup on the floor. "We don't know what we're into here, but the more collateral damage we can mitigate, the better. My guess is that York will be out of it for a while. Maybe even until tomorrow. And it'll be days before he can travel."

"They'll have taken her by then," Mads said.

Roy nodded.

"You really can't be serious," she said. "I need to be here when York wakes up."

"If you're not back, I'll explain it to him."

She cocked her head at him. "*Seriously?* You seriously think he'll just be fine with that?"

Roy ran a hand across his mouth.

"That's what I thought. I don't care what Logan says—you should be the one to go."

"And if Martin shows up?"

She stiffened. "We're on a Naval base. Martin is an international criminal. We're safe."

Roy pursed his lips.

"What?"

"It's not only Martin. We don't know how far this rogue faction in the CIA extends. We can't trust anyone outside the Caleb Group. Logan is right. I need to stay and protect York. You'll have help in Germany."

"What about your friend in Germany? Can we trust *her*?"

"That's different."

She raised an eyebrow.

He met her gaze, his unflinching.

Interesting.

"No," RJ said.

"Yes," Mads said. "Hana will be afraid."

"She'll have you."

He sighed, something troubled in his eyes. "Her mother and I were...we had our differences. I told her not to get involved with the Petrovs, but she was desperate. Hana needed the experimental medicine—and then she got in too deep and...I was so angry. We got in a fight right in front of Hana. I am not sure..." He walked to the window. "I have lost everyone. Everything."

Oh.

She looked at Roy, whose mouth had tightened around the edges. He leaned forward, his forearms propped on his knees, and she had the sense that he didn't sit still often.

In and out in an hour. "How soon can we leave?"

"I can arrange a flight in an hour."

She sighed. Looked at Mads who now stood, his arms folded, staring bleakly out of the window.

Fine. "Call your contact and arrange the flight." She got up.

"Where are you going?" Mads said.

"To tell York what's going on. And I'm praying that he doesn't wake up with a heart attack."

Roy smiled, but she wasn't entirely kidding.

York was asleep in the bed, an oxygen mask cupped over his nose and mouth, an IV attached to his arm, the covers tucked in around his body.

The hospital gown looked positively out of place on his body, stretched over his wide chest, pulling against his strong arms. She ran her fingers through his short, dark blond hair and leaned in and kissed his forehead.

He didn't stir.

"I have to go to Germany," she said. "With Mads. But Roy will be here. I promise, I won't go running after trouble. I'll get Hana, and I'll meet you back here." She had run her fingers down his arm, and now wound them into his hand.

How she wished he'd squeeze it back. Let her know that he heard her.

"And then, we'll go home. Enough of this craziness. We'll buy that house and walk down the aisle and I'll be a soccer mom—I'm sure I can find enough trouble there. And most of all, we'll be happy, York. We'll have a calm, safe, perfect life and we'll be crazy happy."

Her eyes blurred and she blinked back the moisture. "But you have to get better. You have to heal and not do something crazy like die on me, okay?"

Again, no squeeze of his hand, so she did it for him.

His chest rose and fell, steady, even, and maybe that was assent enough.

Then she pulled off her engagement ring. Put it on the bedside stand next to him. "And this is my promise. I'll be back for the ring. For our life."

She leaned forward though, moved the mask, and pressed a kiss to his lips. He didn't respond, but she didn't care.

"I love you, York. I promise, I'll be right back."

Then she put the mask back, watched him breathe for a moment, and walked out the door.

WHAT HAPPENS NEXT...

He'd slept like the dead.

But the smell of fresh coffee roused him from the darkness, and York woke with a start. Light filtered in from a wide window, taken up mostly by the massive hulk of Mt. Etna that rose boldly to the north. A wispy blue sky overhead suggested he'd slept well into the day.

He'd had a rough night, given the pain that circled his body. He shifted, noting the IV that ran in his arm, the cannula under his nose. Maybe he'd had surgery—last he remembered was RJ kissing him on the wet deck of a boat.

No, wait. Something else. But he couldn't close his mind around it.

He followed the smell of the coffee—Roy sat in a chair on the opposite side of his bed, staring into the brew, pensive by the drawn look of his mouth.

Roy wore a clean tee-shirt, a pair of jeans, boots. And he'd shaved. He looked up, probably sensing York's gaze. "Hey."

"Hey."

Roy got up, his mouth pinched. "Glad to see you back among the living."

Something...

York groaned, painfully aware of the burn in his lower back. "Don't get too excited. I feel like I've been mowed over by a Humvee."

A smile lifted one side of Roy's mouth. "You had surgery. Lost a lot of blood."

Ah, that accounted for his winter nap. "Got any more of that?"

Roy looked at the coffee. "Sure. You can have mine." He set the cup on the tray. "I haven't touched it."

"Just holding onto it for moral support?"

"Something like that."

He'd been kidding, but...

The door opened and a male nurse came in. Blond, high and tight cut, built. A sailor in scrubs, his name over the pocket. Peters. "You're awake. Good. I just need some vitals."

He came over and pulled a thermometer from his pocket, sheathed it and stuck it in York's mouth. Then he grabbed his wrist, checked his watch. "You gave us a scare there when you didn't wake up after twenty-four hours."

York stilled. Wait—what?

The thermometer beeped, and nurse Peters retrieved it. Gave a nod and a smile at the results and threw out the sheath. Then he grabbed the blood pressure cuff and tore it open.

York held out his arm. "How long have I been out?"

Nurse Peters wrapped the cuff around his arm. Pulled out his stethoscope. "Um, let's see. You came in after midnight... two days ago? You roused yesterday, but you might not remember it."

Maybe he did. He remembered voices. No, RJ's voice. *Something.*

176

"So, it's been three days, maybe."

Three. *Days.*

Nurse Peters finished taking his blood pressure and unwrapped the cuff. "You were low, but it looks like you might be edging on the high side." He looked at the coffee. "Maybe lay off the strong stuff. But I'll order you some lunch. Soup?"

York just stared at him. "I'm not hungry."

"You need to eat. Keep your strength up." He stepped back. "You want to have energy for when your fiancée comes back, right?"

York looked at Roy, who looked at nurse Peters as if he'd like to...

Oh. *No.* "Where. Is. RJ?"

"I'll take it from here," Roy said. "Thanks, Sam."

The nurse nodded. "I'll order the soup."

The door closed behind him. York stared at Roy.

"Just stay calm."

"You don't look calm."

"She's fine."

"The fact that you have to assure me of that..." And then he heard it—the voice, soft in his memory. *"I'll be right back, I promise."*

His chest nearly seized. "Where did she go?"

Roy held up his hand as if to hold back whatever reaction York might have to his words. Which only fisted York's chest more.

"Germany. To get Hana, Mads' daughter."

York just stared at him. "You sent her to *Germany*? With Martin still out there? Have you lost your mind?"

"No. Listen. We chartered a private jet. She went right to Heidelberg with Mads. Met up with my contact there. Went to the hospital. Picked up Hana."

He took a breath.

Silence.

"And then?"

Roy's mouth tightened. "She, they...they vanished."

A beat, during which the words found his chest, tunneled right down into his soul.

"What did you say?"

"They didn't meet their exfil point."

Still, he was sorting out the words, trying to get a grip on them.

"RJ left the hospital? She—she *left* me?"

"She didn't want to. Mads—he was wild with fear, and you were out of surgery and...it's my fault. I told her that she'd be back in a few hours. Go to Germany, get the kid, come back."

He leaned back onto the pillow. Wow, everything hurt.

"I'm looking for them. I have people on the ground. She didn't have a phone, so I was relying on my contact. It's possible something happened to her, and they went into hiding."

York's gaze jerked up, pinned Roy. "Something happened? Like Martin lying in wait for them, grabbing them and right now torturing the woman I love?"

Roy made a face.

He stilled. "What aren't you telling me?"

Roy exhaled hard. "The other scientist, the one in the van... his name is Ruslan Gustov."

Gustov. "As in..."

"Damien's kid brother."

Yep. That seemed right.

Because the past just couldn't let him escape.

"We'll find her, York."

"Mmmhmm." York reached over and pulled the IV from his arm. Slapped his hand over the blood that oozed from the wound.

Then he eased up, ignored the groan, and swung his legs off the bed.

"What are you doing?"

But Roy's words faded as York's gaze fell on his side table.

Her ring.

He picked it up and something inside him cracked.

RJ, what have you done?

And then the pain inside solidified, turned dark and hard, and everything simply moved to the back of his head, for another time, another place.

York stood up. "What do you think I'm doing?" He reached for the ties of his hospital gown. "Get me my pants."

Find out what happen to RJ, and what York does next in:
I Will Find You

1 WILL FIND YOU

Of course the woman York loves has gone missing. He didn't know why he expected RJ not to chase danger into trouble. But she's in over her head, and he has to find her before criminal mastermind Alan Martin tracks her down.

RJ didn't mean to leave York behind, but she's on a mission to save a little girl caught in the crossfire of Martin's terrorist plot. Now, she'll have to find the girl and keep her safe while leaving clues for York to follow her.

But who will catch up to her first—York, or the man with a vendetta?

A Note from Susie May

Thank you so much for reading *Out of the Night!* I hope you enjoyed the story. If you did, would you be willing to do me a favor? Head over to the **product page** and leave a review. It doesn't have to be long—just a few words to help other readers know what they're getting. (But no spoilers! We don't want to wreck the fun!)

I'd love to hear from you—not only about this story, but about any characters or stories you'd like to read in the future. Write to me at: susan@susanmaywarren.com.

I also have a monthly update that contains sneak peeks, reviews, upcoming releases, and free, fun stuff for my reader friends. Sign up at www.susanmaywarren.com

And, if you're interested reading more epic romantic suspense, head over to https://www.susanmaywarren.com/ genre/contemporary-romantic-suspense/

Thank you again for reading!

Susie May

ABOUT SUSAN MAY WARREN

With over 1.5 million books sold, critically acclaimed novelist Susan May Warren is the Christy, RITA, and Carol award-winning author of over forty-five novels with Tyndale, Barbour, Steeple Hill, and Summerside Press. Known for her compelling plots and unforgettable characters, Susan has written contemporary and historical romances, romantic-suspense, thrillers, rom-com, and Christmas novellas.

With books translated into eight languages, many of her novels have been ECPA and CBA bestsellers, were chosen as Top Picks by *Romantic Times*, and have won the RWA's Inspirational Reader's Choice contest and the American Christian Fiction Writers Book of the Year award. She's a three-time RITA finalist and an eight-time Christy finalist.

Publishers Weekly has written of her books, "Warren lays bare her characters' human frailties, including fear, grief, and resentment, as openly as she details their virtues of love, devotion, and resiliency. She has crafted an engaging tale of romance, rivalry, and the power of forgiveness."

Library Journal adds, "Warren's characters are well-developed and she knows how to create a first rate contemporary romance..."

Susan is also a nationally acclaimed writing coach, teaching at conferences around the nation, and winner of the 2009 American Christian Fiction Writers Mentor of the Year award. She loves to help people launch their writing careers. She is the founder of www.MyBookTherapy.com and www.LearnHowtoWriteaNovel.com, a writing website that helps authors get published and stay published. She is also the author of the popular writing method *The Story Equation*.

Find excerpts and reviews of her novels at www.susanmaywarren.com and connect with her on social media.

facebook.com/susanmaywarrenfiction

instagram.com/susanmaywarren

twitter.com/SusanMayWarren

bookbub.com/authors/susan-may-warren

goodreads.com/susanmaywarren

amazon.com/Susan-May-Warren

CONTINUE THE ADVENTURE

THE EPIC STORY OF RJ AND YORK

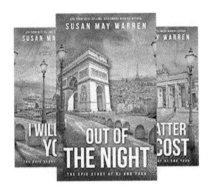

Book 1: Out of the Night

Book 2: I Will Find You

Book 3: No Matter the Cost

Also by Susan May Warren

FIND OTHER EPIC ROMANTIC ADVENTURES BY SMW!

Sky King Ranch

Global Search and Rescue

The Montana Marshalls

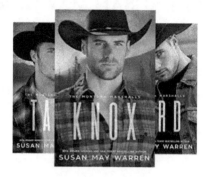

Montana Rescue

Montana Fire

Global Guardians

Out of the Night

The Epic Story of RJ and York series

ISBN: 978-1-943935-59-8

Published by SDG Publishing

15100 Mckenzie Blvd. Minnetonka, MN 55345

Scripture quotations are taken from the King James Version of the Bible.

Scripture quotations are also taken from the Holy Bible, New International Version®, NIV®. Copyright© 1973, 1978, 1984, 2011 by Biblica, Inc®. Used by permission of Zondervan. All rights reserved worldwide.

For more information about Susan May Warren, please access the author's website at the following address: www.susanmaywarren.com.

Published in the United States of America.